HATCHER'S LEGACY

Book 2 of The Munro Family

DEL PRATT

Tellwell Talent
www.tellwell.ca

ISBN
978-0-2288-5243-8 (Hardcover)
978-1-77962-430-7 (Paperback)
978-0-2288-5244-5 (eBook)

DEDICATION

I would like to dedicate this book to Ken and Joan Mick. Two excellent school teachers who taught Sheila and me in high school and who are all round great people. They came to Oyen, Alberta, in 1970 to cover a six-week teaching position…and are still here! A long six weeks! Ken and Joan recently celebrated their sixtieth anniversary. Most days in the summer, they can be found on the local golf course. Sheila and I always enjoy our visits when we meet in town.

ACKNOWLEDGEMENTS

I would like to take this opportunity to thank my wife, Sheila. Her unwavering support and encouragement to follow my dream are big factors in making these novels possible. I can spin a pretty good yarn. But her editing and polishing are what make my mutterings readable.

It's a busy life for a rancher's wife. Sheila tracks all the bookkeeping and banking; makes the preparations for branding, vaccinating, and pregnancy testing the cows; helps check the herd during calving season; hops on her Ace to move cattle between pastures; and feeds a hungry haying crew.

Before Sheila came out to the ranch, my bookkeeping practices included gathering up all of the unopened mail from the back seats of the three farm trucks once a month and taking it into our local bank. The patient tellers helped me wade through the bills and make all the necessary payments (which weren't always done in a timely manner). I'm not sure who was happier—me or the ladies at the bank—when I married Sheila, and she took over the finances!

Between us, I think we make a pretty good team. Glad to have you by my side.

~ Del

AUTHOR'S NOTE

This fiction story takes place in 1867, the year Canada was formed into a country. Well, almost, as we didn't completely become self-governing until the Statutes of Westminster in 1931.

This is also the year that the United States got the deal of the century. Seven million US dollars for Alaska. Two cents an acre.

The United States and Great Britain were in a ten-year-long dispute that ended in 1872. The dispute centred on the warships built in British shipyards for the Confederate states during the Civil War. The Czar of Russia needed cash to help pay for losing the Crimean War to Britain, France, and the Ottomans. There was no way that Russia was going to sell any land to Britain.

Britain and Russia were also in competition in the area north of India. Britain's main reason for being in Afghanistan during the Anglo-Afghan War of 1839 to 1842 was to keep Russia away from India.

I added a taste of these international intrigues into my story.

Captain John Palliser's expedition was from 1857 to 1860. He mapped the southern half of Western Canada.

This included the forks of the Red Deer and South Saskatchewan (Bad) Rivers, as well as the Cypress Hills. I have a copy of Palliser's map and used it extensively while researching for this book. Palliser even mentioned the grizzly bears on the South Saskatchewan and the rattlesnakes.

My account of the land is as authentic as my research could place it. Bears were a real factor on the prairies in the 1800s. In 1871, 750 bear skins were traded out of the Cypress Hills to the Hudson Bay Company.

Dinosaur hunting was certainly within the realm of possibility, as the Hall Expedition led by paleontologist Fielding B. Meek in 1854 had found fossils in southwest Dakota.

The hot, dry weather on the prairies was more commonplace in the 1700s and 1800s than even today.

Enjoy the story! I hope it tweaks an interest in Western Canadian history.

~ Del

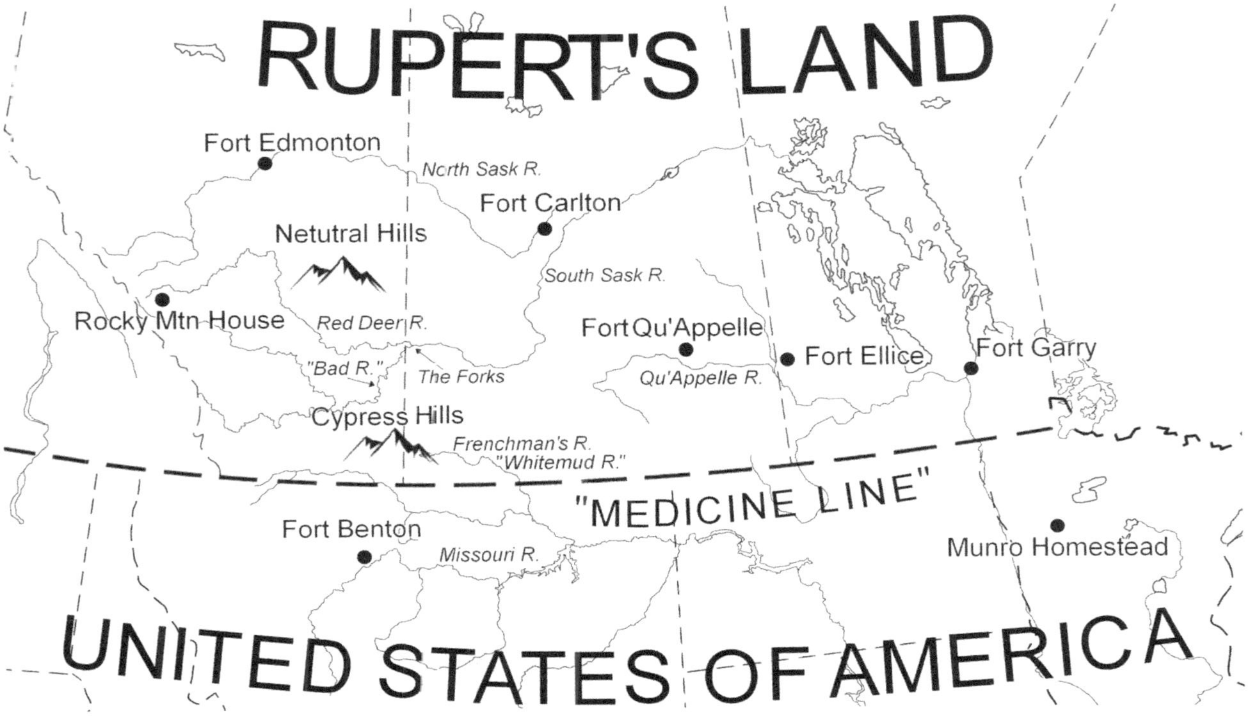

RUPERT'S LAND
UNITED STATES OF AMERICA
"MEDICINE LINE"
Fort Edmonton
North Sask R.
Fort Carlton
Netutral Hills
South Sask R.
Rocky Mtn House
Red Deer R.
Fort Qu'Appelle
Fort Ellice
Fort Garry
"Bad R."
The Forks
Qu'Appelle R.
Cypress Hills
Frenchman's R.
"Whitemud R."
Fort Benton
Missouri R.
Munro Homestead
Map designed by Chengis Javeri

GLOSSARY

Alyeska – The archaic spelling of Alaska.

Arroyo – A steep-sided gully formed by fast-flowing water in an arid or semi-arid region. In the area covered in this book, these were formed by water from melting glaciers in the last Ice Age.

Ashley's Men – The first mountain men to go west and trap for the Rocky Mountain Fur Company circa 1822.

Battle of Inkerman – A bloody battle in November of 1854, during the Crimean War, which resulted in a British victory.

Bell tent – a circular canvas tent with a central pole, stabilized by ropes and stakes.

Brackish – Water not fit to drink.

Breech-loading – A gun that is loaded at the rear of the gun barrel.

Buckshot – Small round pellets made of lead.

Buffalo waller – Mountain man slang for a buffalo wallow, a natural topographical depression in flat prairie land that can hold rainwater and runoff in wet years.

Bull boat – Made by covering a skeletal wooden frame with a buffalo hide.

Butt plate – A metal plate covering the butt (end) of the rifle.

Calibre – The measurement of the width of a bullet, or a round lead ball, in one-one hundredths of an inch.

Carbine – A firearm with a shorter barrel—usually around twenty inches long—which was issued to the cavalry.

Cartridges, metallic – A metal case made of brass or copper that contained the primer, the gunpowder, and the bullet. Used in the breech-loading guns which came out during the Civil War.

Cat tracks – Footprints left by a mountain lion, also referred to as a cougar.

Coulee – A deep ravine.

Coup d'etat – An overt attempt by military or government elites to unseat the current leadership.

Crimean War – A war fought from October 1853 to February 1856 in order to curtail the expansion of the Russian empire and preserve the Ottoman Empire to maintain the balance of power in Europe.

Double ought buckshot – One of the larger sizes of buckshot.

Farrier – A craftsman who trims and shoes horses' hooves.

Flintlock – A firearm that uses a flint-striking steel to create a spark to ignite a small amount of black gunpowder in a pan on the outside of the gun. This causes a small flame to enter a little hole in the barrel, which ignites the main charge. Flint guns date back as far as the 1500s and were the main ignition system up to the 1820s.

Furniture – All of the metal on a muzzle-loading rifle, except the lock and the barrel.

Go Under – To die.

"Good Book" – The Bible.

Green River knife – A favourite of the mountain men, these knives were made in Greenfield, Massachusetts, by J. Russell.

Grubstake – To lend a prospector money or provision for a share of the resulting proceeds.

'Hawk – Short for tomahawk.

"Hell-bent for leather" – To ride a horse as fast as it can gallop.

Hobble – To tie the front legs of a horse together close enough to prevent it from straying away.

Iron Confederacy – A political and military alliance of Plains Indians: Cree, Salteaux, Assiniboine, and the Metis; as well as Iroquois who had come west with the fur trade.

Jasper – Old-fashioned slang for a fellow or a man.

Leech and Rigdon – A Confederate Civil War revolver copied from the Colt Navy.

Lever action – A firearm that uses a manually operated cocking handle located around the trigger guard area to feed and extract cartridges into the chamber.

Lineback dun – A light cream-coloured horse with a primitive mark that's darker than the base colour, resulting in a stripe down the horse's back.

Lion – Another term for a mountain lion or cougar.

Magazine – A place where the cartridges are stored in a repeating rifle.

Magnetic observer – A person who uses a compass for navigation.

Medicine Line – How Indians referred to the border between the United States and British North America.

Muzzle – The front end of the gun barrel.

Navy Colt – A .36-calibre handgun manufactured by Colt.

Nazareth mountain rifle – These were large .54-calibre rifles with full length stocks, produced by various gunsmiths around Nazareth, Pennsylvania. They were used by the mountain men who went west to trap beaver circa 1820. These rifles could weigh up to fourteen pounds.

Oneida – One of the tribes of the Iroquois Six Nations.

Pan flash – One of the drawbacks of a flintlock gun was that, at times, the priming powder in the pan would ignite but would fail to ignite the main charge in the barrel. This is where the saying "a flash in the pan" comes from.

Passel – A large group of people or things.

Percussion cap (commonly referred to as a cap) – A small copper or brass cylinder with one closed end. Inside the closed end is a small amount of a shock-sensitive explosive.

Picketing – Tying a horse to a tree or stake with a long rope so it can graze freely.

Pierre's Hole – A shallow valley in Eastern Idaho, just west of the Teton Mountains.

Pilgrim – A greenhorn, new to the land.

Pistol – A handgun.

Powder charge – The amount of gunpowder used to fire the gun.

Ramrod – A long round rod used to push balls down the barrel of a rifle or for cleaning the rifle barrel.

Rattlesnakes – Venomous snakes living in the Western Hemisphere, characterized by a segmented rattle at the tip of the tail that produces a buzzing sound when vibrated.

Reb sniper rifle (also referred to as Whitworth sniper rifle) –A rifle made in England patented by the Whitworth Company in 1854 and issued to Confederate snipers. The interior of the barrel was hexagonal with a twist and used a corresponding hexagonal bullet, thus causing their bullets to make a distinctive whistling sound.

Red River cart – Wooden two-wheeled carts made entirely without metal. The mainstay of wheeled transportation in Rupert's Land.

'Ree – How mountain men referred to the Arikara Indian tribe.

Remuda – A herd of saddlebroken horses.

Rendezvous – An annual summer gathering in the Rocky Mountains, where the fur trappers and Indian tribes could trade and exchange goods with the trading companies.

Revolver – A handgun that commonly has one barrel and uses a revolving cylinder containing multiple chambers for firing. Often also referred to as a six-shooter.

Rifle musket – The most common weapon of the infantry soldier in the American Civil War. It had a thirty-seven to forty-inch long rifled barrel with an average weight of nine pounds. They included Springfields, made in the USA; Enfields imported from England; and the Lorentz, imported from Austria.

Rifling – Spiral grooves cut inside the barrel of a gun to make the bullet spin, thereby improving accuracy.

Sam Hill – Slang for 'the devil' or 'hell' personified.

"Seeing the Elephant" – Civil War soldiers referred to being in combat as having "seen the elephant."

Sextant – An instrument used in celestial navigation to measure latitude and longitude by determining the angle between the horizon and a celestial body such as the Sun, Moon, or a star.

Sign – How mountain men referred to clues or tracks left behind from what or who had been there before them.

'Skeeters – Short for mosquitoes.

Smoothbore musket – Older guns that were still in use during the Civil War, with smooth barrels that had no rifling.

Spencer carbine – One of the first practical repeating carbines. The magazine held seven rounds and was located in the butt stock.

Stock – The wooden part of a gun to which the barrel and firing mechanism are attached. On older military weapons, the stock went the full length of the barrel.

Surrey – A light horse-drawn four-wheel carriage with two seats facing forward.

Swale – A low or hollow place between ridges.

Trade musket – Smoothbore flintlock muskets traded to the Indians by the Hudson Bay Company and American traders for over two hundred years.

Travois – A type of sledge used by North American Indians to carry goods, consisting of two joined poles pulled by a horse or large dogs.

Wagon – Horse-drawn vehicle with four wheels. Many of the parts were made of metal.

Warner Carbine – One of the many single-shot breech-loading carbines that came out during the Civil War.

York Factory – A large Hudson Bay Company post located on the Hays River, where it flows into the Hudson Bay.

PROLOGUE

LAND OF THE NORTHERN SHOSHONE 1831

Under the lower boughs of a tall spruce tree lay a trapper. Although only a young man, not yet thirty, his long hair was snow white. He was dressed for the cold in a buffalo coat and beaver hat. However, after crawling through the knee-deep snow and then lying still, his body was starting to feel the chill. He wasn't a big man, maybe five foot four, but with a strength and determination that far surpassed his stature. Whatever needed doing would have to be done soon though, or his hands would be too cold and stiff.

He now peered over a snowdrift that had formed around the tree. His penetrating blue eyes were focused on a small encampment. It was about two hundred and seventy-five yards across a large clearing, slightly downhill and east from where he lay.

Spring had come early, and the trappers had been out setting traps in the beaver streams. Then this cold snap had hit with a blast of arctic air coming down from the north country. With it came a heavy snowfall.

Before the winter had returned with a vengeance, a Blackfoot raiding party out to steal horses had entered

Shoshone territory from the east. Horses were considered the measure of wealth for most tribes. Unfortunately, they had caught two of his friends. He'd found Smiley dead and scalped. From the cuts and burns on his body, it wasn't hard to tell that he had been tortured before he'd died. Hatch had been captured and was now tied to a tree and being mercilessly tormented. His screams could be heard by the white-haired trapper even before he had crawled through the snow to get under the tree.

He was too late! Hatch was beyond saving. He had been tortured for too long. All that was left for him in this life was more pain from his tormentors.

As a warrior took a glowing stick from the fire and was taunting the prisoner by pointing it at one eye and then the other eye, Hatch screamed out, "DO IT, MUNRO. DO IT!"

The white-haired trapper brought up his heavy Nazareth flintlock and rested it on the hard snowdrift. The air was crisp and cold with no wind. Wiping the tears from his eyes, he cocked it, took aim, and squeezed the trigger. He hardly heard the loud blast of the rifle as it spat forth a fifty-four calibre round ball. Across the clearing, it made a sickening thump as it bore into his friend's chest.

Bolting up, the trapper ran through the snow to his horse. There was no sense in hiding now; the smoke from the black powder was a dead giveaway as to his location. He was on his roan Appaloosa and heading south within seconds.

Behind him, the Blackfoot warriors howled in shock and anger. Quickly recovering, they ran to their horses, ready to chase after the trapper. However, their leader stopped them. They already had the stolen Shoshone horses, and catching the trapper who spoiled their fun wasn't worth heading back farther into enemy country. Why take the chance of running into a bigger bunch of very upset Shoshone warriors?

It was the next morning when the tired trapper met his Shoshone friends who were in pursuit of their stolen horses. Both man and beast were too worn out to join them. In the end, the Blackfoot got clean away.

When he was rested, Munro went back and cremated what was left of his friend. For the rest of his life, he would remember the sound of the ball hitting Hatch in the chest. But it was the torturer's face that haunted him in his nightmares. For as he was squeezing the trigger, the brave turned, showing the red whiskers of a white man!

Part One

The Expedition

CHAPTER ONE

God, it was hot! The midday prairie sun was bearing down and drying everything out even more than it already was. Any way you cut it, sliced it, or diced it, we were in trouble.

My bay mare didn't have much left in her, and Celine's buckskin was almost done. Moses's Appaloosa was still game, but not for long. We had to find a place to hole up real soon, or that bunch of warriors on our backtrail were gonna catch us. Judging by the mood they appeared to be in, it wasn't a social visit they were a'wanting either.

Moses's long white hair flowed out from underneath his old plainsman hat as he topped a small rise. Raising his arm, he pointed to a small grove of chokecherry trees growing out from the centre of an old buffalo waller.

We rode right into them trees and managed to find a pathway to the middle. Here was a small clearing, just big enough to hold our horses. Hopefully, there were enough bushes and trees to stop bullets from hitting our mounts.

Moses grabbed his tomahawk and started hacking into the ground. "Jim, stand guard on the edge while Celine and me scrape us out some cover!"

Celine started scooping out dirt with her Green River knife while Moses moved to a new spot. When he was done chopping through the undergrowth and topsoil, he started digging as well.

I kept a close eye on our surroundings. We could have been in a far worse spot. There was open ground all around us, the only problem being the rise to the west that we had rode over to get here. Some riflemen could lay just at the crest and shoot down at us. They'd be mighty hard for us to hit.

Moses came over to me. "I'll watch for a bit if you can help Celine get them rifle pits a little deeper."

"You bet," I answered my grandfather.

Going over to where my wife Celine was digging, I got on my hands and knees and started hollowing out more dirt. "If Moses and me can hold them off for a bit, you might be able to get away once my bay has had a bit more rest."

Her dark brown eyes flashed back at me as she shook her long black hair out of her finely sculpted face. "Non, Monsieur Munro! For better or worse, remember. We either all make it out of this, or we all go down fighting."

What she lacked in size was more than made up for with steadfast courage. As Old Moses had said on our wedding day, "I knew that gal was a 'keeper' from the first day we met her!"

I smiled to myself, thinking back to that first encounter when she had been holding a knife to my throat!

Grinning, Moses turned towards me. "Looks like you lost that round, Jim. We better get ready. Looks like our friends have arrived."

I got Pa's field glasses out of my saddlebags and started looking over our pursuers. I counted sixteen. Something didn't look right, but what? They sat on their horses on that knoll about three hundred yards to the west, watching us. One of them dismounted on the left side of his horse and got a spyglass out of his saddlebags. *Left* side! It hit me: "That's a white man!"

Moses responded, "Darn right it is. Any Indians I ever knew mounted their horse from the right."

"Oui," Celine chimed in. Being Metis, the first language she had learned was French. When stressed, she at times reverted to it.

"They seem to be looking us over pretty good. Do you think they know about these Spencers we're packing?" Moses asked.

"Doubtful," I answered. "How many could have made their way this far north?"

I kept watching them through the field glasses. The feller with the spyglass had blond hair. I could see him look at Celine and grin. It would be over my dead body before any of that crowd would ever lay a hand on her. Then I could tell he was looking at Moses. He sized the old man up for over a good two minutes before putting his spyglass away.

"Moses, he was mighty interested in you. Take a gander at him." I handed the glasses to my grandfather.

Moses studied the figures on the hill for a couple of minutes before handing the glasses to Celine, saying, "I'm a thinkin' some of those riders are Indians, but I can't tell what tribe."

Celine studied the riders for a minute but shook her head. "There's nothing familiar about them. Something's just not right."

I looked at Celine and Moses. "No, it ain't. I think we just may have found MacTavish's troublemakers. Even so, we can't wait here all day. Our horses need water, and our canteens will be empty before long. We have to make something happen. Moses, why don't you take a shot with your carbine but hit the dirt about a hundred yards ahead of them? Give me a few seconds to trim a branch that will make do as a ramrod. After you shoot, pretend you're reloading a muzzleloader. That might bait them into attacking us, and we can open up with these repeaters. If they get close, we still got our revolvers."

Moses waited until the stick was ready. Then he nodded while raising his Spencer. "When they get within two hundred yards of us, open up on 'em."

Moses fired, and his bullet hit a good hundred yards out in front of our enemies. Celine slid into her rifle pit and prepared to fire. I stood by my pit, wanting to get a good clear shot at the leader before I followed suit and dropped my six-foot-one frame into the small depression we had managed to scrape out.

The dismounted rider laughed as he climbed back on his horse. Then, giving an order, he led the charge.

Moses dropped the fake ramrod, then levered a cartridge into his carbine and pulled the hammer back. Celine's and mine were already cocked. When the attackers' horses reached where Moses's first bullet had hit, we opened up on them.

I had the leader in my sights. When I fired, he flinched in the saddle and dropped his rifle. Then it felt like the world slowed down, and all I could hear was the roar of gunfire. Over and over, I levered my Spencer, aimed, and fired at hazy targets until my carbine was empty, and I tossed it to the side. Dropping into my rifle pit, I drew my Leech and Rigdon pistol and continued shooting through the cloud of black powder smoke into what remained of the riders as they thundered on past us!

Then, all was quiet. The acrid smell of burnt powder hung heavy in the hot, dry air, and smoke stung our eyes.

I called out, "Celine, are you alright?"

"Oui, I am not hit," came her reassuring reply from my right.

To my left, I could see Moses snap open his Spencer's butt plate and start feeding cartridges into the magazine, so I knew he was okay. By now, I was thumbing in my seventh cartridge into my carbine, and Celine was reloading as well.

In front of us were two dead horses and three bodies. Ten yards past Celine, another body lay face down in the dry prairie grass.

"Another one over here; he's dead," Moses hollered. Even though we were only a few yards apart, we were yelling so we could hear over the ringing in our ears.

Celine had been keeping an eye out to our rear, where the riders were now regrouped about four hundred yards away. Suddenly she cried out, "They're getting ready to attack again!"

Moses's head snapped around to look back while I kept a watch on our dead enemies, just in case one wasn't as dead as he let on.

"Jim, they think they're safe that far away. What say we raise these sights to four hundred yards and put the fear of Mr. Spencer into 'em?" Moses shouted to me and Celine.

After re-setting our sights, I called out, "Okay, let's give it a try. We'll all fire off two shots as fast as we can!"

We raised our carbines. I counted us down—three, two, one—and we squeezed the triggers. Then, we levered in new rounds, firing again before we even knew if we'd hit anything with our first shots.

It took a few seconds for the smoke to clear, but what a sight. We had caught them off guard at that distance. Two of the riders had been piled off when their horses had spooked. One horse had been hit, and another man lay motionless on the ground.

Something clicked in my head, and I yelled, "Down!"

All three of us dove into our rifle pits just as a bullet whined over right where I had been standing. I swung up my carbine and snapped a shot at the man lying behind the dead horse out in front of us. As he raised his head to take aim, both Celine and Moses fired. One of them drilled him dead centre.

Spinning around, I could see the remaining riders charging at us again, already less than two hundred yards away. All three of us opened up, and when our carbines were empty, we fired what was left in our pistols.

As quickly as it had started, the fight was over. What was left of our attackers were heading west as fast as their tired horses could carry them.

I called out, "Celine? Moses?"

"Oui," my wife answered. "I'm fine."

"I'll be alright," Moses gasped.

I immediately spun towards him and saw that he was bleeding from a wicked cut on his left cheek.

"Got another nick on my left arm too," he heavily breathed out the words.

Celine was already at his side, ripping the sleeve off Moses's plaid shirt to reveal a deep gash.

Moses spoke up; we could all hear a little better now. "Don't you worry, I'll be fine. Just get the horses and reload all the guns. We need to be ready in case those jaspers come back. And Jim, check out those carcasses. We gotta figure out why white men are disguising themselves as Indians. Might give some answers as to why they were so hell-bent on trying to kill us."

I headed into the trees and soon came back, leading our horses. Luckily, none had been hit. Like us, it wasn't their first shooting scrape. But they still needed some time to calm down.

After reaching into the saddlebags for another box of cartridges, I reloaded all three Spencers. Thank God and Caleb Daniels for these guns. We'd have gone under without them today. I also took the time to reload all three of our pistols. That took a little longer than the rifles, as our pistols were cap and ball revolvers. We'd captured them while rescuing my sister, Judith. That was a couple years back when some deserters from the Civil War made off with her. By the time we got her back, them fellers we took the pistols off of didn't need them anymore.

While I looked after the guns, my wife set to work patching up Moses. She always carried a small bottle of rubbing alcohol with her, as well as a needle and thread.

The dry prairie grass crunched under my feet as I walked over to inspect the fallen attackers. As I surveyed the battlefield, I counted nine dead. I was pretty sure we had also wounded some of our would-be killers.

The first body I looked at was the jasper behind the dead horse. Even though he was a white man, he was wearing Indian clothing. He'd been armed with a trade musket, which wasn't unusual. Indians had been trading for muskets for over two hundred years. As I checked out the other men, another mystery appeared. Not all were white men. Six were darker skinned, but not any tribe I was familiar with.

After Celine had sewn Moses up, I called her over. "Have you ever seen a tribe with features like that?"

"Non," she replied with a puzzled tone. "These men have dark skin, but their features are different from any Natives that I have ever seen. The leatherwork on their clothing is different as well. These men are not from any Plains tribe or any Woodland tribe that my family traded with."

"Well, we'll have to ponder this, I reckon. All of them were armed with Hudson Bay trade muskets, but that's to be expected. We'd better head back to camp. Hopefully we can find some water before nightfall. The horses need it bad, and our canteens are low. Guess we'll just leave the muskets. The horses got all they can carry as it is."

We mounted up and started heading northeast, back to the camp of our employer, Professor Sir John Jacob Augustus Martindale the Third.

Celine took the lead as we rode east. Being Metis and raised on the vast prairie by traders, she had an immense knowledge of the land we were travelling across. She had figured we were roughly half a day's ride east of the forks of the Red Deer and the South Saskatchewan Rivers. It would take a long day of riding to reach the camp of Sir John, as our employer preferred to be called. It was already late afternoon, and we had to find water and a place to camp for the night. In this heat, water was the be-all and end-all.

It was quiet as we rode, other than the creak of leather and the swish of our horses swatting flies. We were all winding down from our brush with death. There was also the very real possibility that our new "friends" would come back with re-enforcements. We were a long way from being out of the woods yet. If we didn't find water for the horses, we were going to be on foot for as long as our canteens lasted. And that wouldn't be long!

As we doggedly made our way, I found myself thinking back to how we came to be in this situation.

Chapter Two

Two years ago, my sister Judith had been abducted by a gang of renegade deserters, left over from the recent war between the states. Moses, Pa, and myself had trailed after them and eventually saved her and brought her home. Along the way, we rescued Celine, the girl who became my wife after we got home to Minnesota. It was Celine and her knowledge of the land that had made it possible to free Judith.

Once we were home, Pa sent a letter to Caleb Daniels telling him what had happened and all we had done to get Judith home. He and Pa had served together in the war. When the hostilities had finally ceased, Pa returned home, but Caleb had stayed in the army as an intelligence officer. It was he who had sent Pa a letter to be aware of some deserters possibly heading our way.

It turned out that the US government was right pleased with how we had handled that situation. We had virtually wiped out the renegades and had done it on good terms with the HBC governor in Rupert's Land as well. Way we heard it, there were people in Washington who wanted to give us medals, but Caleb had a better idea.

And so it was that a wagon, escorted by a squad of cavalry, rolled into our yard in the late spring of 1866. A young lieutenant rode up to Pa and me, asking, "Would you be Captain William Munro, sir?"

"I am, Lieutenant. What can I do for you?" answered Pa as he looked over the small party of horse soldiers. They had been on the trail for a few days, but these were professional soldiers. Unlike the rabble we had dealt with last year, this unit had pride in their appearance. All were clean-shaven, and other than sweat stains, their uniforms looked cared for. The carbines slung on their backs looked well-maintained. All were mounted on bay geldings with clean and well-oiled McClellan saddles. This was an outfit!

"Lieutenant Brent Hastings, sir. I bring a letter from Major Daniels and a box with some new Spencer carbines and seven hundred and fifty rounds of ammunition. His letter explains everything. If you will show us where to unload the wagon, we can get on our way back to Saint Paul to catch a steamboat back to Washington."

Pa told the soldiers they could unload the guns and ammunition on our front porch. We would take care of them.

An Irish sergeant named McGilvery had the troopers unload all the crates. Once this was done, the cavalrymen watered their horses and filled their canteens. Pa signed a paper for the lieutenant, and in a matter of minutes, the horse soldiers were back on the trail.

I went to our little blacksmith shop and brought back a prybar to open the crates. When I pried the top off of the first crate, we were greeted with the sight of six brand new Spencer repeating carbines!

"My Lord," gasped Pa. "I only saw a few of these in the last year and a half of the war. Most were shipped out to

Billy Sherman's cavalry in the Western Army. Jim, these are a piece of modern machinery. Seven shots before reloading, and they take the same cartridge as our Warner carbines."

About then, Moses drove our wagon in the yard. He was returning with Grandma and Celine after taking them over to Ollie and Judith's new house so the ladies could have a visit. The couple had only been married for a few days before the renegades had descended upon their homestead, injuring Ollie and capturing Judith. After we had found Judith and brought her back home, the couple hadn't felt secure living far away from us and so had moved to a new farm site only a mile away.

Moses and the ladies walked up to the steps and looked at the gleaming new guns.

"Those from your friend Daniels?" Moses queried.

"Yup," responded Pa. "Six new Spencer carbines and seven hundred and fifty cartridges."

"He expecting us to fight a war?" inquired Moses. "That's a lot of expensive hardware in them boxes."

Now, at the time, I'll admit I didn't really think much of it. As far as I was concerned, we had pretty much fought our own war last summer, and I wasn't looking for another one.

While Grandma and Celine fixed supper, the three of us men cleaned the grease off the new guns. We figured one each for Pa, Moses, Celine, Ollie, Judith, and myself. We had lots of cartridges so we could practice and get used to them.

Some might wonder at our womenfolk packing these carbines. But after last year, there was no way that either of those two young wives would ever be unarmed. At least not in our immediate future.

Thankfully, we had managed to have a rather uneventful year for the rest of 1866. We put up feed for our stock and harvested oats and some wheat. In the fall, there was a good shindig over at our neighbours, the Olsens. One of their daughters had married a new settler in the district. Things were downright getting peaceable. You might say, even civilized. Celine and I had been discussing where we might like to get a place for ourselves where we would hopefully be raising our own family.

It was in the spring of '67 that things started to unravel on the farm. Spring had come early, but the rains had not. Old dead growth from last year was abundant. The whole district was a tinderbox waiting for a match.

When the fire started, it wasn't a match, though. It was a dry lightning storm west of us a few miles. Moses noticed it first. He was out at the corral that evening, checking on a mare that was due to foal within the week. The horses were restless, whinnying and shaking their heads. Even the usually calm milk cow was antsy.

That's when the old man caught his first whiff of smoke. A prairie fire and it was coming right at us! Very faintly on the horizon was an orange glow.

Moses started hollering, and we all came outside to see what the ruckus was.

Pa took one look west. "Jim, harness both teams and get the wagon and the hayrack hitched!" He could see Moses had already caught the riding horses and was saddling them as fast as he could.

Grandma and Celine started packing up food, then began gathering the dishes and wrapping them in clothes. Pa ran back in the house and came out with an armload of carbines, which Moses grabbed and put in scabbards as he saddled horses. Ammunition and our extra rifles were put in the wagon.

By now, the horses were getting harder to work with, and the smell of smoke was strong. The orange glow on the horizon was starting to show flames reaching for the sky.

We had the wagons hitched and loaded: dry goods, staples such as sugar and flour, blankets, utensils, guns, and the few blacksmith tools we could easily grab. Horses without riders were tied to the wagon or the hayrack. The whole time, the fire was getting ever closer, burning and devouring everything in its path.

Pa yelled out, "Time to go!"

We tore out of the yard, heading north. Celine drove the wagon with Grandma sitting beside her while Pa drove the hay rack. Moses took point, and I brought up the rear, keeping our milk cow, Bossy, with us.

Soon we were at Ollie and Judith's place. They had been busy packing all the earthly possessions they could into their wagon. With our extra hands, we finished loading them in minutes. And then our little cavalcade was rolling north as fast as we dared take the wagons.

All the while, the smell of burning prairie grass and trees was getting stronger. We could see the flames reaching higher and higher as they got closer. Fortunately, the breeze was light, and although the fire was coming towards us, we figured we were going to make it.

Pushing ourselves and our stock to the limit, we kept going north. Even though everyone had tied a wet bandana or scarf over their face, we all were coughing and hacking. It was hell on the stock, but we had no choice but to keep driving as hard as we could. The sun had set, the only light coming from the orange blaze of the all-consuming flames. We managed to keep everyone and everything together through it all, with the horses, mule, and even the milk cow keeping pace. By the time the rising sun started to glow in the eastern sky, the flames were behind us. With the wind dying down, the fire had slowed and would burn itself out when it came to a good-sized stream or lake.

To the west, it was clear, with no smoke or flames. We came to a pond and finally felt safe to make camp. We had survived. All we had in the world was in these wagons. But as Moses said, "I started out with a hell of a lot less."

Once we all had a long drink and the stock was watered, we filled the two water barrels we had managed to save. Then we all jumped into the pond to wash the smoke off our clothes and ourselves.

Grandma, Judith, and Celine dug through the wagons to come up with fixings for a meal. Moses, Pa, and I picketed the horses, Rosie, the mule, and Bossy out to graze. We knew we were going to have to rest for a couple of days to let the stock recover. As rough as this had been on us, it would have been even more so for the animals.

We hunkered down for the next two days. Thank God we had had time to gather a lot of the things we needed most before the fire chased us away from our homes. With some tarps, we had been able to set up a fair to middling shelter. This kept us reasonably warm and dry when it started to rain the second afternoon. If there were any embers still smouldering from the fire, the rain would put them out.

As we huddled under the tarp, we took stock of our situation. What to do now? Our seed stocks were gone, and any feed we had on hand was burnt up. Our machinery, such as it was, was damaged beyond repair. The barns and corrals were gone; there was nothing to return to.

Pa looked around at us as Judith poured a round of coffee. "There's not much to go home to. Actually, things are worse now than when we first settled. At least there had been grass for the stock then. With nothing left to graze for over two days, counting both ways, we can't even go back to see what's left. In a couple of months, there might be enough growth to go back and figure out what we can salvage. We don't have a lot of options at this stage of the game."

Looking across the fire at Pa, I couldn't help but notice how gaunt he was getting. He never had been what you would call heavy. His shoulders had been broad, though, and his arms and legs had always been strong. When Pa went off to the war, he'd been all of six feet tall. To me, invincible. Now, I was looking at a man aged beyond his years. His hair was greyer, he was bent over when he walked, and I doubt he even weighed a hundred and forty pounds. It was his coughing that worried me most of all. The rest of us had quit coughing hours ago. Pa hadn't.

I glanced over at Celine. She gazed back at me, concern on her face, and I could tell she had been noticing the same things as me. Looking around our small circle, I could see we were all worried about Pa.

Moses broke the silence. "Lookin' like our best option is to head north to Fort Garry and see if we can pick up some work. Maybe haul some freight with the wagons or some kind of a job for the Bay. At least we're on good terms with the governor."

"There is even a need occasionally for translators," offered Celine, "and between Moses, William, and myself, we can get by in seven, maybe even eight languages."

Then Grandma spoke up. "I think it's in the cards for us to head north. Moses, I know you never would have said that you wanted to go back to Rupert's Land. But I can see the yearning for new trails in your eyes. Jimmy, I see the way you look north when you think no one is watching. Celine, you can't hide the fact from me that you would like to see your homeland again. We have nothing to go back to, so my vote is that we go north."

Ollie and Judith exchanged a long look. She nodded back to him before he voiced his thoughts. "It looks like we're heading north with you. There is nothing left at our place either. Maybe it's time for a fresh start."

With all in agreement, as soon as the rain stopped and it was dry enough to drive the wagons, we headed north to Fort Garry and Rupert's Land. Once a decision is made, it seems as if a lot of the stress fades away. Would we ever be back to our farms in Minnesota? Only time would tell.

Chapter Three

Two and a half weeks after the fire, we were looking at MacDougal's dilapidated scow of a ferry coming towards us from the Fort Garry side of the river.

Once the boat landed, Pa went over and negotiated our passage across the Red River.

"I can't believe that contraption is still floating," grumbled Moses.

"Good thing it ain't noon yet. Gonna take quite a few trips," I replied.

"You all crossed on this wreck before?" Grandma commented in disbelief.

"We did. Twice," Moses answered drily.

By now, Pa was back and had figured out all of the logistics of crossing. "Jim, you take the wagon across first. Next, Ollie will follow with theirs. I'll be takin' the hayrack on the third trip. Ollie and me will stay with the wagons and stock on the far side; Jim will come back. Moses will bring Grandma, Judith, and some of the horses. Jim and Celine can follow up with the last horses, Rosie, the mule, and Bossy, if she'll come."

Despite the precarious condition of the scow, the crossing went reasonably well. After having the ferry go back and forth for a number of trips, there was just myself, Celine, my bay mare, Rosie, and, of course, Bossy, the milk cow. Having put a halter on her, I figured to lead her onto the ferry. She had other plans and they didn't include being led anywhere!

"Well, Bossy, guess we'll have to sell you to someone on this side of the river." I untied the halter and walked onto the ferry. The ferryman started to pull out when suddenly there was a thump and a clatter. Bossy apparently decided that she'd followed the horses this far, so she may as well stay with them and somehow managed to jump on that ferry on her own!

We were almost across when the cow jumped off. She managed to swim the last twenty yards and drag herself up on shore. Shaking herself off, she started to graze as if it was just a normal day. We had crossed the Red River.

Pa looked us all over. "We're here. I reckon we could check in with Mr. Affleck at the general store."

Ollie stayed back with the wagons, saying, "I'd better stay and keep an eye on things. Wouldn't want the horses straying or anything."

We agreed, and the rest of us made our way through the gates of Fort Garry and over to the trading store in the southeast corner. We had made the acquaintance of the storekeeper, Charles Affleck, during our rescue of Judith a couple years back.

When we entered the store, it was just as packed as it had been on our previous visits. Hardware, guns, dry goods, bolts of cloth, and pants and shirts of various sizes were piled high on the shelves. He even had one of those Singer sewing machines that had come out recently. I'd seen advertisements for them in the *Harpers Weekly*.

There were also sets of harnesses and a couple of saddles. And we knew that there were farm implements and wagons stored in an outdoor shed. If this place didn't have it, you probably didn't need it!

The storekeeper warmly greeted us, speaking in his Scottish brogue. "Munros, it's good to see you folks again. I hope you're not looking for another family member."

"No, it's not anything like that at all," replied Pa. "We were burnt out by a fire. Started west of us, by lightning strike, we figured. We had to head north to save our hides. The fire took everything. There's nothing left to go back to and no graze for any of the stock. Seemed to us our best option for now was to head up here and look for work. Once we have a grubstake, we'll consider our options."

"Aye, word of the fire preceded you by a few days. The freighters had to make a wide detour around the burnt-out area. A rider was sent back here so the cart brigades could plan accordingly." Looking at Grandma, he asked, "Is there anything I can get you, ma'am—any canned goods, cloth, needles, or any utensils? If you need any of those items, let me know. The Bay can cover it. Your family saved Rupert's Land a heap of trouble when they took care of those renegades. I feel we still owe a debt of gratitude."

"Thank you kindly. I'll be back another time, once we're settled in somewhere," answered Grandma.

Moses interjected, "We appreciate your kind offer, Mr. Affleck. But right now, what we need more than anything is a good place to set up our camp. Preferably somewhere our stock could graze and get rested up."

"It's pretty much settled for miles along the rivers. I do have a pasture that I rent out to travellers for their stock. I'll give you a deal on the grazing, and you can set up your camp there. When you're ready, you could go west and find some open land to set up a more permanent camp," advised Affleck. "I'll send a message to Governor MacTavish, letting him know you are here. I suspect he'll want to talk to you folks."

Then he took out a piece of paper and drew a map to find his place. He handed it to Pa, saying, "Best of luck to you folks."

Even having been here before, this massive fort still impressed me. The surrounding walls were fifteen feet high and made of stone. Within the enclosure were multiple warehouses and living quarters built two stories high.

And all the activity! There were farmers, traders, and Indians from various tribes, all conducting their business. There was a constant parade of Red River carts, coming and going. Some were bringing in furs from the forts out West, while others carried produce from the fertile farms along the rivers. Then there were the carts loading up with supplies or commodities to ship out to the many forts, including Ellice, Qu'Appelle, Carlton, Pitt, and Edmonton. Yet other carts were exporting goods down to Saint Paul in Minnesota.

We made our way out through the huge stone archway, back to where Ollie was waiting with the wagons. "Looks like as much activity here as there was in some of the big centres in the east during the war," commented Ollie. Like Pa, Ollie had fought through the war and seen a lot of combat. As he once remarked to Pa, he had seen all the elephants he'd ever want to see.

"It's a big area that this place is the business centre for," commented Moses. "I can think of at least three forts within three weeks riding supplied from here, and at least five tribes' worth of trading that passes through here. And that's just to the west. I reckon there's some business to the east as well."

Following Affleck's directions, we made our way west on a trail for close to an hour. Stopping at a survey stake, Pa held up his hand. "Looks like we turn south here. According to his map, the property starts at this stake and goes straight down to the Assiniboine River. It runs west about three hundred yards along the river bank. We'll make camp close to the river, and we can picket the livestock back a ways from the camp."

We surveyed the treeless plain and then decided to set up a tarp shelter between the wagons. After eating a meal of bannock and tinned peaches, we sat around the fire doing some figuring. No solid ideas came out of this. We would have to see what transpired after our meeting with the governor. We settled down that night, grateful to have made it safely that far.

Morning brought another warm, sunny day. Maybe a little too warm for early May, to my way of thinking. We'd just finished watering our horses and were in the process of hobbling them when we heard the sounds of a horse-drawn carriage. I turned to see a black canopied surrey making its way towards us!

A team of matched grey geldings was being driven by the governor's nephew. We'd met him a couple years back when we'd passed through these parts. Sitting in the back seat was Governor MacTavish and a lady who I figured must be his wife. She appeared to be a Metis woman, like my wife, Celine.

As I watched him climb down from his rig, I could see that the governor was showing his years. He had developed a cough and was looking even more run-down and tired than he had two years ago. But he still had a firm handshake as he reached out and greeted us all while presenting his wife, Mary.

Although they had heard much about this man, this was the first time Grandma and Ollie had met Governor MacTavish in person. Once the introductions and pleasantries were over, he got down to business. He addressed Pa, saying, "It is my understanding that you and your family are looking for some form of employment."

"Yes. We will need to make a living and get a grubstake in order to either rebuild or relocate to another place," responded Pa.

The governor half smiled with a twinkle in his eye as he asked, "Would you consider guiding a professor from England on a dinosaur hunt?"

Moses burst into laughter and asked incredulously, "You want us to help some Englishman find and dig up old bones?!"

"Ah, so you know what dinosaurs are. That's good," declared MacTavish. "That makes it easier. All I know is what Sir John has told me. Ferdinand Hayden found dinosaur bones on the upper Missouri in 1854 while on a partially funded geological expedition for the Smithsonian Institute. The good professor has been talking to traders and Indians from out West. He is of the opinion that the eroded sandstone cliffs along the Red Deer River valley would be a promising place to explore."

Moses replied, "Ah, I knew Hayden's guide. We both went west with Ashley's men."

It was Celine who voiced what Moses and I were both thinking. "Monsieur Governor, it is perhaps not my place to interrupt. But does this Englishman realize that is Blackfoot territory? We got lucky once, two years ago, in our encounter with some Blackfoot, because they decided they needed to hunt buffalo in order to feed their people more than they needed to fight us. I don't think we could count on getting so lucky again."

MacTavish pondered for a moment. "I think it would be reasonably safe if you went to the forks of the Red Deer and the South Saskatchewan Rivers. Richard Hardesty's dispatches from Rocky Mountain House have been indicating that the Blackfoot are farther west. He's become a good friend of one of the band chiefs; I believe his name is Crowfoot.

"I have been authorized by the HBC board of governors to pay good scouts or guides a hundred pounds sterling for the job. That's per person, mind you. That would be well over six hundred Yankee dollars each for three of you."

"Why don't you give the job to some of the locals?" I wondered aloud. "Surely they need the money."

MacTavish replied, "Most are already out on the spring buffalo hunt. It seems that they are having to travel farther afield to find enough buffalo. Some are away trading as well. I know of a couple of good guides who would be available in two weeks. But Sir John wants to get started as soon as possible."

Pa had stepped back from the discussion when he had broken into a cough. He was attempting to muffle the sound with his sleeve, but we could clearly hear him. I realized that, if anything, Pa's cough was getting worse.

Grinning, Moses looked over to where Celine and I were standing. "Want to go looking for some old bones with me?"

I turned to Celine and asked, "What do you think?"

Without hesitation, she replied, "Oui, our family needs the money. And I know that country. William?"

Pa paused. Then, with a long, meaningful look at Moses, he shook his head. "I reckon I'll sit this one out."

I was surprised to hear Pa say this but realized he was right. He had come home from the war weakened. The need to be constantly riding and living outside for all those years had taken its toll. He had only been home a few months before Judith was abducted, and we had headed out on the trail of her kidnappers, not finding her until late fall. Even two years later, Pa was still run-down. He needed a rest.

Governor MacTavish directed his comments to Moses, Celine, and me. "Excellent! I will let Sir John know that he has guides. He may not like the idea of a young woman scouting, but I will personally vouch for Celine. I know fully well how capable she is."

The governor then turned towards Ollie and Judith. "Ma'am, how well can you read and write?"

When most people looked at Judith, they saw a tall, pretty, shapely girl with long blonde hair and deep blue eyes. But she was way more than that. She was intelligent and resourceful, and it was no surprise to me that the governor could see what was there.

Grandma had made sure that both Judith and I had some schooling at home. "I can read and write very well, sir," answered my sister. "And also do arithmetic as well."

"Excellent, we lost a school teacher at the fort last year. She married some ne'er-do-well from Canada, and they 'pulled stakes' and went back east. The job is yours if you want it. A cabin goes with the position, so you and your husband can have a roof over your heads."

Then, looking at Pa with knowing eyes, he said, "Mr. Munro, I understand you were a captain in the army. My chief trader needs assistance in keeping track of the inventory. I have room in my home for you and your mother while you are working in the fort."

"Mr. Johansen, I can see by your hands that you've worked with them a lot. What did you do before you started farming in Minnesota?"

Ollie responded, "I was a soldier in the Union Army. Before the war, I was apprenticed to a carpenter in the old country. I can build buildings or make furniture if that would be useful."

The governor looked pleased. "Can you repair buildings? Or make shingles or doors? I could use a good man for full-time maintenance. My repairman died last fall, and I haven't yet found a replacement for him."

"Yes, sir. I will do whatever is needed," Ollie declared solemnly.

Then Grandma piped up. "Governor, what can I do to help? I may be getting old, but I can still carry my share of the load."

"Well, Mrs. Munro, we do have a lot of children who need schooling. Would you be willing to work with your granddaughter at the school?"

"I was a school teacher many years ago. I can certainly help Judith. Thank you, Governor."

"Mr. MacTavish," I asked, "What do we do with the horses that we won't be needing on our guiding job?"

"That won't be a problem," replied the governor. "Your extra horses and cow can come up to the fort and run with the Bay's animals. We have a young man watching them so they don't stray too far. At night, they are put in a paddock close to the fort. Your wagons will be safe as well."

Then, looking at Moses, Celine, and me, he said, "I will speak with the three of you tomorrow morning to brief you on the details of your expedition. Say 7:30."

With that, the governor nodded to signal an end to our conversation. Then he and his wife climbed back into the surrey and started making their way back to Fort Garry.

We looked at each other, almost in shock at how quickly our fortunes had changed from the talk with the governor. Then Pa said, "Well, we had best break camp and head to the fort."

The rest of our day was spent packing up our camp and moving Ollie, Judith, Pa, and Grandma into their respective lodgings. Moses, Celine, and I also spent the night at the governor's residence.

That night as I lay beside Celine, rather than falling asleep my mind was busy thinking about what was to come. How long would we be out West on this expedition? Would we really be able to help the professor find actual dinosaur bones? And what would happen after the expedition? Would we ever be going back home to Minnesota? Or was our future to be up here in Rupert's Land? I finally drifted off into an uneasy sleep.

Chapter Four

It was 7:30 when the four of us met outside MacTavish's office. Late last night, the governor had sent word that he would like Pa to be present at the meeting as well. Pa's knuckle had barely rapped on the door before it was opened, and we were shown into the inner sanctum of the HBC and the Red River Colony. The governor's nephew was there to take notes of the meeting.

"Gentlemen," MacTavish started. Then, smiling at Celine, he added, "And Mrs. Munro the younger. I'll get right down to business. A dispatch rider from Fort Edmonton arrived last evening. He was carrying word of unrest among the Natives over a large area of the plains.

"Richard Hardesty, the trader at Rocky Mountain House, has passed on some information. As I had previously mentioned, he has become friends with some of the Blackfoot. One of them told him that there was talk of war among some bands. Someone is travelling around, visiting the various tribes and spreading lies.

"The Blackfoot and Cree are always one step from open warfare. What I don't understand is who would benefit from a war. The buffalo are getting harder to find, but there is still plenty to go around for now. If there comes a day when the buffalo are scarcer, then fighting will break out. And not just among the Blackfoot and Cree. Assiniboine, Saulteaux, and a host of other tribes will be hungry. That is in the future, though, and currently, I have to deal with the present.

"I have also been made aware that the Plains Cree are not happy with there being so many white men in their territory. However, I have managed to secure safe passage for the expedition with the help of a mutually respected Metis trader. As a gesture of goodwill, the Bay will pay out two hundred pounds in trade goods to the Cree at Fort Carlton.

"Most of your journey will be through Assiniboine country. And as I understand it, you are on good terms with them.

"Keep your ears open and find out if there is any truth to these rumours of misinformation and unrest. You may not have heard yet, but the eastern colonies have agreed to form a dominion, which would basically be a self-governing country under Queen Victoria. With wealthy Canadians, rather than the British, now being the major shareholders of the Bay, the West will be changing.

"There are already people in parliament pushing to have Rupert's Land sold or turned over to Canada. It wouldn't take much for a troublemaker to stir up an uprising on the plains.

"As much as I sympathize with the Natives, wars between themselves or against the white man will not help anybody. Nor will it stop the manifestation of what is going to happen. There is no doubt in my mind Canada will be taking ownership of Rupert's Land in five years or less. And then, settlement of the West will become a major initiative.

"In light of all this new information, with your permission, I would like to reinstate your special constable commissions. If something untoward does happen while on this expedition, you would all be acting as my representatives."

Moses pondered, then asked a question. "I reckon we could do that, but what do you want us to do with Sir John if we do hear of trouble?"

The governor responded without hesitation, "Turn him and his cavalcade of carts around and bring him home. Especially at this time, a dead rich Englishman would make diplomacy on the plains even more complicated."

MacTavish then turned to Pa. "William, you will be working with the chief trader at the fort. I will see to it that you have time to ride around the settlements and get to know the people. Some of the Metis move around trading and hunting, even though they live here at the fort. Any little pieces of information you hear could be important."

Speaking to Moses, Celine, and me, he advised, "I will give you a letter of introduction for Sir John." His glance lingered on Celine. "I want you to know there could potentially be more risk than originally planned."

Celine met his eyes squarely and determinedly spoke up. "Where Jim goes, I go. Besides, I'm the one who knows the country well."

The governor had a slight smile on his face as he responded, "I suspected you might feel that way. But I wanted to be sure that you were aware of the risks before agreeing, in order to ease my conscience."

Then his nephew handed the governor a sheet of paper to sign. Passing Moses the signed letter of introduction for Sir John, he said, "As for Sir John, you might find him not too bad of an employer. He appears to take the welfare of his men seriously. Affleck said he bought a lot of supplies, enough to feed his crew for weeks. All you will need to take with you are your guns, ammunition, and bedrolls." He then shook our hands, wished us luck, and we left the office.

Moses, Celine, and I packed up our gear. Then we met up outside the governor's residence to say our goodbyes to Pa, Grandma, Judith, and Ollie. Grandma hugged each of us tightly. I was sure Judith had tears in her eyes, although she quickly wiped them away. Ollie shook our hands with a solid grip and a steady gaze. Pa looked sombre, and I could tell he was wishing he was going with us. But he also knew his health wasn't up for the trip.

Six horses were tied to a hitching rail waiting for us, having already been fed by a Metis lad. Once saddled, we led our spare horses out the north gate of the fort. We followed the Carlton trail northwest for roughly a half hour before coming across the camp of Professor Sir John Jacob Augustus Martindale the Third. There was a flurry of activity. Tents were in the process of being struck, and everything was getting packed away in the carts.

"Looks like Sir John travels in style," I commented as we looked over the camp.

Moses pointed out, "Must have close to twenty people counting us. Six bell tents, a full brigade of ten carts with hoops and canvas covers, drivers, and a remuda of spare riding horses, not to mention the oxen for the carts." He continued, "I don't see many guns, considering we're headed for the wilderness. Those cart drivers will likely be carrying trade muskets, but I don't see much else."

"There's something familiar about one of those Metis fellas over by that last cart," I mused.

"Oui!" Celine excitedly agreed. "It's my cousin Leonard Trottier!"

"By God, that makes me feel better," spoke up Moses. "We'll have some good help babysitting these greenhorns. Those cart drivers won't be no pilgrims, either."

"Reckon it's time to get acquainted with Sir John and his crew." I started my horse towards the camp, with Moses and Celine following closely behind.

It wasn't hard to see who the leader was. He was as tall as me but slightly heavier, with a balding head and spectacles. I'd never seen a professor before, but he fit what I had imagined. I was surprised to see that Sir John was helping pack his own tent. He looked up as we approached. "You must be the scouts MacTavish promised. Jolly good timing." Then he exclaimed, "Bloody hell! MacTavish said he would hire scouts, and I get a young girl and Methuselah?!"

"Sacre bleu," hissed Celine, amongst a tirade of French words I hadn't picked up yet.

I could see a grin breaking out on Moses's weathered old face. I think even Sir John was getting her drift.

"Mister, I'm Jim Munro. You wanted scouts, and you got three of the best. That young girl is my wife, Celine. She was born two days east of the Cypress Hills twenty years ago on a buffalo hunt. She knows that country as good as anyone. Two years ago, she led Moses and myself across over five hundred miles of wilderness to the Yellowhead Pass. And got us there in time to save my sister. That 'Methuselah' is my grandfather, and he was wintering in the Rocky Mountains before you were even born. He could part your hair with his Green River before you even blink. Between these two, they speak seven tribal languages as well as Sign Talk. I'm a thinkin' you need us a hell of a lot more than we need you!"

Looking Sir John in the eye, I demanded, "Do you want scouts or not?"

Sir John stood back and seemed to study us in a new light. "My god, you're the Munros! I heard stories about you at the fort. You rather put an end to what amounted to a small invasion of British territory. Please accept my humble apologies. I would be very pleased to have you as scouts.

"We had been told to expect you to arrive this morning. And as you can see, we are striking the camp. Another half hour and we'll have the oxen hitched, ready to roll. Would you like to meet my staff?"

"Not right now," Moses spoke up. "We want to have a bit of a parley with the cart drivers. We can all get acquainted when we make camp tonight. You can call me Moses. Everyone else has for the last forty-five years."

By now, most of the carts were hooked to the oxen that would pull them. Each ox was tied by a lead rope to the cart ahead of it. This way, three men could manage ten carts, which was called a brigade.

Not a piece of metal was used to build these Red River carts. Wood and buffalo hide were the main components. The spoked wheels, five to six feet in diameter, were mounted on axles made of oak. No grease was used on the hubs, as it would catch dust and grit from the dry prairie and wear the axles quicker. This meant you could hear the squealing carts a mile or more away on a calm day.

A Red River cart could be pulled by a horse or an ox. A horse could travel faster and farther in a day but hauled less than five hundred pounds of freight. An ox, while travelling slower, could pull between nine hundred and a thousand pounds. With all the camp tents, supplies, and long boxes of digging tools, these carts easily exceeded what a horse would be able to pull.

Weaving our way through the milling people, we finally caught up to Leonard.

"Bonjour, Leonard," cried out Celine, loud enough to be heard over the organized confusion of people cramming the entire camp into ten carts.

Leonard spun around sharply. "Celine!" Then, seeing Moses and myself, exclaimed, "Moses, Jim, you are the scouts we have been waiting for? Bien! I can help you out when I'm not needed with the carts."

"Sounds good to us," I responded. "At least you will know the route if we're out ahead scouting. Who are the other cart handlers?"

"The Sinclair brothers—Mark, Luke, and John. They've been hauling freight for the Bay for years. Good men. Some of the best cart drivers around. If we run into trouble out there, they'll stand their ground; they've been in a couple of scrapes with the Lakota."

"What's your take on Sir John?" Moses questioned.

"For an Englishman, he is not all that bad. I think ten loaded carts is a lot of cargo to haul around looking for bones that have been buried for centuries. But what do I know? I have never looked for or dug up dinosaurs before. Watch his assistants when we set up camp tonight. I'll let you figure for yourselves about them."

Moses then nodded to me. "Looks like the carts are loaded and hitched. What say we start earning our wages?"

Mounting up, we rode towards Sir John, who was on a white horse at the head of the column.

"A white horse?" Celine snapped, still not cooled down on the subject of Sir John. "Is he trying to show how brave he is, or is he just another English fool?"

"Either way, we're paid to lead him out to the forks," I answered her.

"Don't forget about finding dinosaurs," chuckled Moses.

Approaching Sir John, Moses called to him, "We'll keep following the Carlton trail. We're aiming to cover fifteen or sixteen miles today. We're close to the Assiniboine River, so we can stop midday for a break and to water the stock."

Sir John looked up from his conversation with one of his men and nodded. We rode past him and trotted on ahead to take the lead. Our expedition was underway.

CHAPTER FIVE

Once on the trail, we could hash things over amongst ourselves. Until we were past Fort Qu'Appelle, our job would be mainly scouting for good campsites and water. The trail was easy to follow as it had been in use for years. Once we were off the beaten track and out on the plains, then we'd be earning our wages. Leonard and the Sinclairs also knew the country well, so would always have their bearings. We would be scouting for miles around the cavalcade, looking for anything that could pose a problem. Even finding water that wasn't in our direct path was knowledge that could come in handy.

"We're going to have to start scouting out from the trail tomorrow," voiced Moses. "If there is anything to the reports from out West, we best be in the habit of looking the country over for five or six miles around the carts. Might even have to drop back and see if anyone is following. It's probably no big secret that an expedition is heading west. If I was a troublemaker, this is a prime target."

"It wouldn't take much of a lie to say Sir John is doing a survey before the white settlers move in," I commented.

"There has already been a survey to look over the land for settlement," responded Celine. "My family met them out on the plains close to the Cypress Hills when I was twelve. I think the boss man was named Palliser. We only traded for a while and stayed one night with them. I remember my father talking about it with other traders. No one was too happy about the idea of white settlers from the east pouring in like a swarm of locusts."

"Can't say all this wild country gettin' settled and put to the plow pleases me, either," growled Moses. "I'm old enough I won't see much of it, but it will happen."

We rode well ahead of the carts for the rest of the day. Midday was spent by a small lake that still had water that wasn't brackish yet. If it didn't rain soon, this was going to be a mighty dry trip, especially when we made it out west of Qu'Appelle.

The rest stop seemed to go over well, as far as we could tell. The cooks, who were wives of two of the cart drivers, had bannock and pemmican for the midday meal.

Once the animals had rested, the procession carried on, following the trail. Even though the dry grassland we were riding through seemed flat, the swell of the prairie could hide a horse and rider just a mile away. The only trees in this area were the cottonwoods along the banks of the Assiniboine River to the south of us. Mounted on fresh horses, the three of us spread out to look for signs of horse tracks. I rode off to the southwest while Moses went northwest in a loop. Celine stayed on the main trail.

By late afternoon, the three of us had joined up again at a small creek. It wasn't much more than a trickle but would do for an overnight camp. We sat on our horses as we watched the carts and riders coming towards us. Two Metis boys were driving the remuda of spare horses.

We indicated to Sir John where we wanted the camp, and within forty-five minutes, the last bell tent had been set up. The carts, as always, were arranged in a circle to protect against attack. Some of the horses were hobbled inside the circle while others and the oxen were hobbled nearby. We were taking no chances on animals straying away during the night.

The Sinclair ladies wasted no time preparing a meal. After eating a supper of fresh bannock and soup, we sat around and drank tea, which seemed to be the main drink in these parts.

At this time, we met the six men Sir John had hired as labourers. They were there to help pack and unpack the camp. If we ever found a dinosaur skeleton, they would be the ones working with Sir John to exhume it. Moses told me that he'd heard that sandstone had to be carefully chipped away from the bones. It could take hours, or even days, to do this, depending on the size and number of the bones.

Duncan Alexander seemed to be the foreman of the outfit. He was a heavy-set Scot of average height with greying reddish hair who looked to be in his late forties. His deep brogue could be heard booming around the whole camp. As Moses drily commented, it wasn't the first time he gave orders.

Jonesy Harris seemed to be next on the ladder. A tall, dark-haired, slim man, he kept an eye on the carts as they were being loaded. He appeared to be sociable enough when spoken to, but seemed to spend most of his time alone.

Darragh O'Riley was the farrier and in charge of the well-being of the horses. A big dark-haired Irishman who never seemed to get worked up or riled at anyone, he struck me as a good man to have on our side when the goin' got tough.

The remaining three men—Quincy Adams, Becker Wright, and Isaiah Williams—all appeared steady and reliable.

The Sinclair family seemed to be a decent bunch of hard-working people. They were Metis, descended from Scottish traders and their Native wives. They had been in the freight business for a long time. They owned the carts and oxen.

Two teenage lads, Paul and Gerald, rounded out the crew, being the wranglers for the remuda. Being young, they were excitedly looking forward to their first big adventure.

Admittedly, this was the biggest group of people I had ever become acquainted with in my life. Celine seemed to fit in well with the crowd, although some of the Englishmen couldn't figure out how a girl could be a scout and guide. I reckon they'd never heard of a Shoshone woman named Sacagawea who had guided Lewis and Clark through the Rockies back in 1805.

Moses wandered back to the fire. He had been out doing a little walk around, checking on the stock. I got up when he nodded to me, and we went over to where Sir John was sitting.

"Would you have a minute, Sir John?" I murmured. "We need to discuss something in private."

"Something serious?" he asked, speaking low. He got up from his camp chair and followed us out a ways from the camp.

"I say, is there a problem already?" he questioned.

"Not yet," I replied. "But we have to get people used to being on guard duty at night. If people start taking shifts now, they will be accustomed to it by the time we pass Fort Ellice. Once we get out west past Fort Qu'Appelle, we'll be off the beaten track, so to speak, and on our own."

"Oh, we won't be having trouble with anyone," Sir John airily responded. "The governor paid for our safe passage. We'll be quite safe."

Moses broke off Sir John. "No, MacTavish sent trade goods to some of the chiefs of the Plains Cree in return for allowing your expedition access to their territories. But not all Plains Cree follow those chiefs. And you need to know—the main activity, after hunting on the plains, is horse stealing! You have enough horses here to attract every warrior for God knows how far around. Some young braves could sneak up and leave with a half dozen horses, and you wouldn't even notice until morning."

Sir John countered, "But won't you people be on watch?"

"We can't be on guard all day and all night. And there will be times that we'll be out scouting and be out of contact," I explained. "Out here ain't like university. If you fail, you either lose your horse or worse, you go under."

Sir John peered over his spectacles at us. "Well, this is certainly more than I expected, but I will follow through on your recommendation. I will get Mr. Alexander to set up a watch rotation."

"A word to the wise: have Trottier and the cart drivers give their opinion about when they do their shifts," advised Moses. "We'll do guard duty tonight and you can take care of this tomorrow."

"There's one other thing we need to discuss. Do your men have any guns?" I asked

"I have a pistol, and there's a trade musket in one of the carts. We're a scientific expedition, not a military one. Besides, you people and the cart drivers have guns. I'm a university professor, not a gunfighter. All we want to do is locate petrified bones and take samples back for scientific study," concluded Sir John.

We left the professor at his tent and walked around the encampment until we found Leonard.

"How'd things go with the 'boss man'? I'm thinkin' you asked if he had any guns? I was down that trail myself. Hopefully, we can get him to some bones and get him back alive," he commented.

"Englishmen," muttered Moses. "How in Sam Hill did they ever conquer an empire? It sure wasn't done with the likes of him."

I spoke up. "We did get him to agree to set up a night watch. He will be asking your input tomorrow. But without guns, I'm not sure what they will do if some horse thieves do show up."

Leonard offered, "He did buy a trade musket at the fort. I could at least teach some of them how to load and fire it during our noon time breaks. At least they could look armed if thieves show up."

"You still got that Reb sniper rifle?" I asked. Pa had given Leonard a Whitworth rifle, a capture we'd acquired when rescuing my sister.

"Yup, it's in a cart. I carry my trade gun most of the time. Let me know if you need it."

Moses nodded. "Sounds good. If one of your men takes first watch tonight, we'll do the last two. Once you and Sir John get something worked out, we'll help out when we can. But we'll be leaving early in the mornings to ride out ahead."

Bidding Leonard good night, we went to our tent. Celine had our bedrolls laid out for us. We filled her in on the discussions with Sir John and Leonard, then got what sleep we could.

Two and a half hours later, I was up for my shift. Walking around in the night gave me time to think. I was relieved that Pa, Ollie, Judith, and Grandma were safe for now. But what would our family do for the long term? Celine and I had often talked about wanting to start our own place to raise a family. Was it worth going back to Minnesota? Or was the real opportunity to stay here in Rupert's Land?

I thought back on our conversation with Sir John. He honestly seemed to have no idea of the dangers we could face. Could he really be that naïve? Yet his men seemed to have mastered the art of making and breaking camp awful quickly. Something wasn't quite adding up.

Moses relieved me and took the last shift, which was uneventful. After washing down a breakfast of oatmeal with scalding tea, the three of us set out for the day's scouting. We followed the same pattern as the day before, separating to cover a wider area.

If things went well, we would be at Fort Ellice in ten days, weather permitting. A heavy rain would slow us down considerably. Mind you, it was looking like the odds of that happening were mighty slim.

It crossed my mind how much slower we were travelling this time on the trail. Two years ago, we were pushing forty to fifty miles a day, riding hell-bent for leather after my sister's abductors. Now, with a cart brigade and seven greenhorns, we were hoping for twenty. Once everyone was used to the routine, if we had a good day, we might make twenty-five.

The expedition adjusted to the trail quicker than we had expected. Sir John and his crew had learned how to stay on a horse. Some even rode rather well after a few days in the saddle. Alexander reminded me of someone, but I couldn't put my finger on who. It was easy to tell that he was more experienced than the others. And he could ride.

Nine days after leaving Fort Garry, without any major wrecks, we led our carts into Fort Ellice. This was more of a traditional fort with a log palisade. It was still impressive, with warehouses and a large building where the trading took place.

We had our midday stop at the fort. The Sinclair wives picked up more supplies, all paid for by the Hudson's Bay Company. I found myself wondering about this. Why would the Bay spend so much for a chance to find some old bones?

An ox had gone lame and was changed out. Two carts needed axles replaced, a common occurrence with wood turning in wood. Sir John seemed to have everything in hand, so Moses, Celine, and I went to the store and looked up McCrimmon. He had been promoted to chief trader since we had seen him. He hadn't changed much. His beard had gotten a little greyer, and he'd gained a little weight.

After hearty handshakes all around, he asked, "What can I be a doin' for you? I see you're guiding yon professor."

"We are," explained Moses. "He's on a dinosaur hunt. Any chance you've heard of any of these old bones being found?"

"Interestingly enough, I have heard snippets here and there. I worked at Rocky Mountain House, oh, I reckon going on twenty years ago. There, we traded mostly with the Blackfoot, Sarcee, and the Stoney. I remember one of the Blackfoot chiefs talking about some ancient skeletons being visible in the Red Deer River Valley."

"Any chance this was close to the forks of the Red Deer and South Saskatchewan?" I queried.

"No, it was way west of there. Way they talked, it was well within Blackfoot territory," the old trader answered.

"Maybe we can get lucky this side of the forks," Moses commented.

I drew out my constable commission. "On another subject, Governor MacTavish also wants us to keep our ears open for anyone travelling around out West trying to cause trouble. Maybe even trying start a war between tribes. I understand it wouldn't take much to get one started between the Cree and Blackfoot."

"Aye, I've heard the rumours myself. Who would gain from starting a war between the tribes?"

"I reckon that's what he's hoping we find out," stated Moses.

Saying our goodbyes, we left the trader. The three of us then made our way to a small cemetery just outside the fort. It was here, overlooking the north bank of the Assiniboine River, that Celine's parents and brother had their final resting place. They had been murdered when Celine was snatched by the same renegades that had kidnapped my sister. We had actually rescued Celine first, and it was because of her that we had been able to save Judith.

When Celine was ready, we made our way back inside the fort. By now, the carts were ready to roll, so mounting up, we led the cavalcade out of the fort.

Sir John rode up to me on his white horse. "I say, would you mind if I accompanied you this afternoon? I would like to see more of the surrounding countryside."

"I reckon you can for this afternoon. But we'd prefer to be on our own after this. It's easier to watch for trouble and to not be seen by others as a single rider." I then added, "If you do end up leaving the cavalcade in the future, you have to leave that white horse behind. It shows up on the prairie for miles. Once we get close to the forks, we'll be trying to avoid attracting attention."

"But he is a good horse!" Sir John protested.

Celine, who still wasn't impressed by Sir John, spoke up. "It doesn't matter how good your horse is if you are dead! And I don't care if your horse gets you killed, but I do care if one of us gets killed because of your horse!" She gave Sir John a glare that would've curdled milk.

She then smiled sweetly at me, saying, "I will see you this evening," and rode off up the trail.

"I get the impression she doesn't think highly of me." Sir John was annoyed. "I'm the one in charge here."

"You may be in charge of this expedition, but you ain't getting anywhere without her. Me and Moses could get you to The Forks alright. But she knows where the good water is, and once past Qu'Appelle, it gets even drier.

"If we find there are no Blackfoot around, we could look for dinosaur bones a few miles up the south side of the South Saskatchewan River Valley southwest of the forks.

Celine knows the country around that area. She speaks four Native languages plus Sign Talk. If or when we run into Indians out here, you will need her to translate." I continued, "She grew up in a world where a mistake could get you killed. You treat her with the respect that she deserves, and she might get to tolerate you."

Sir John was quiet as we rode out southwest from the carts.

We had stopped to give the horses a rest on a low-rising knoll about mid-afternoon. Taking Pa's field glasses from my saddlebag, I scanned the horizon in all four directions. I was ready to put the glasses away when I caught the tiniest bit of movement to the southeast, a long way off in the distance. It was gone as quickly as it had appeared, with no dust.

"I say, did you see something?"

"Not sure," I answered him. "Probably nothing, but it's best not to take a chance. We'll lead the horses off this knoll and then mount up. Time to mosey over to the trail and catch up to Celine. She'll be at tonight's campsite by now. The carts may even be there ahead of us. We pretty much follow the Qu'Appelle River to the next fort."

Supper was already being served when we arrived at the camp. Sir John left me and rejoined his men for the evening meal. This gave Celine, Moses, and I a chance to compare how things had gone out on the prairie.

Moses grinned as he asked, "Interesting day with His Lordship?"

"Could've been worse," I responded. "Once I explained how much he needed my wife to find his dinosaurs, he stayed reasonably quiet. He's got a lot to learn, but there may be hope for him yet." I continued, "I did notice movement off to the southeast but could've been a buffalo or anything."

Moses nodded his head. "Could be. Celine, you see any tracks on the trail?"

"Nothing recent. Some unshod horses came from the north and followed the trail at least a week ago, if not more. Could be a hunting party heading west."

Moses looked west, his eyes following the trail. "That may well be, but we can't be certain. I crossed their tracks too. Hopefully, they've moved away from the cart track. We'll have to keep on the lookout."

After supper, Celine and I went for an evening walk around the camp. As we moved past a cart, we heard a hiss. It was Leonard. Looking around to make sure we wouldn't be overheard, he softly said, "Got something to show you, and it ain't good. Take a look under this cart."

I dropped down to my knees to see where he was pointing. There was a cut in the axle.

I kept my voice low. "That's been made with a saw of some kind! A few more days and that axle will snap in the middle. Who on earth would do that?"

"Has to be one of Sir John's men," answered Leonard. "I've known the Sinclairs for over twenty-five years. They would never do something like this. They are good people."

"I know them well, too. They've been in the freight business for a long time. Plus—it's one of their own carts," voiced Celine.

"The boys are usually with the horse herd. So that leaves one of the professor's crew. They've all been on watch, multiple times." I pondered a bit. "Question is, how do we find which one?"

"I can brace this with a piece of wood and some rawhide in the middle of the night. Can you keep whichever of the Englishmen are on watch away from the carts?" Leonard asked.

"I can say I heard something out beyond the horses and ask the feller to go with me. If he is reluctant, we have a possible suspect." I added, "Moses and I are both carrying constable commissions for this job. Governor MacTavish was worried about someone trying to start a war out West. This cut axle makes me wonder if he thought there might be more to this outfit than it appears."

Leonard looked thoughtful for a few seconds. "I have heard rumours of troublemakers travelling from tribe to tribe. Even talk of getting a war going between the Metis and tribes. But I have not seen any of this for myself, though."

Bidding Leonard goodnight, we made our way back to our tent. One of the Sinclairs was taking first watch, so Celine was off of guard duty tonight. We lingered outside our tent, enjoying the peacefulness of each other's company.

Then Celine shook her head. She paused in deep thought before asking, "What if someone snuck into the camp to cut the axle?"

"It's possible," I responded. "Moses once told me a story about a man out in the mountains. Seems he went to sleep with his horse's lead rope in his hand, 'cuz he knew there were Crows around. When he woke up, all he was holding was his rope. A Crow had come in and stolen his horse in the middle of the night. Even though Moses was on decent terms with the Crow, he always claimed they were the best horse thieves in the mountains. So I guess someone that good could have slipped into the camp without us noticing. Or it could even have been done at Fort Ellice when we were all otherwise occupied."

Moses was already sleeping by the time Celine and I ducked into our tent and crawled into our bedrolls. I closed my eyes, but it was a while before I was able to get to sleep. The discovery of the cut axle weighed heavy on my mind. Why would someone want to sabotage a scientific expedition? I couldn't help but wonder what might come next.

Our plan for the middle of the night went off without a hitch. I was on watch with Isaiah. He readily followed me outside the camp to check on the horses. As we headed back towards the circle of wagons, we met Leonard. He looked at me, then nodded, so I knew he had been able to fix the axle.

The next few days were uneventful. The carts squealed their way across the prairie as it got hotter and drier. A solid routine had the expedition functioning like a watch, and there were days we covered upwards of twenty-five miles. Travelling close to the river as we were, good campsites were available with wood and water. Once we passed Fort Qu'Appelle, however, we would be travelling a few days through dry lands away from any river. We would not be near a large body of water until we reached the South Saskatchewan.

Ever since Leonard had found the partially severed axle, we had scouted farther afield. Even riding out fifteen miles away from the carts, we didn't come across anything untoward. But we continued to remain on alert.

I could not shake the nagging thought that all was not quite as it seemed with Sir John. At first glance, he seemed to fit the idea of what an English professor would be like—he spoke like an educated man and was always asking questions. But even though he tried to hide it, he could ride a horse like he'd been born in the saddle. And he and his men seemed to enjoy an easy familiarity, definitely more than I would have expected from a crew who had just been put together for this expedition.

And, it had finally struck me who Alexander reminded me of. The way he gave orders to his men was very much in the same manner as the cavalry sergeant who had brought Pa the carbines from Caleb Daniels.

CHAPTER SIX

Two days before we reached Fort Qu'Appelle, our luck changed. I had reunited with Moses and Celine after a full day of scouting. But there was no sign of the carts; we couldn't even hear them. What on earth had happened to them? Our only course of action was to ride back towards our morning camp in hopes of meeting back up with the cavalcade.

We found the carts just two miles west of where they would have stopped for the noon break. Leonard, who was in the lead, was the first to meet us, a sorrowful expression on his face.

"Problems?" I asked as he came alongside.

"Oui," he sadly replied. "Paul, one of the young horse handlers, is dead. It looks like a horse kicked him in the head. It must have been when he was checking a horse's hoof. I guess accidents can happen, but those boys grew up with horses. They could ride before they could walk. Handling horses was second nature to them. It doesn't make sense to me that he would have gotten caught off guard like that."

"He was an orphan, wasn't he?" questioned Celine.

"Oui. I hired him myself for this job as the kid needed work to survive. His folks were killed a couple of years ago hunting buffalo in Lakota country." Leonard shook his head in disbelief. "Now he is gone. With this heat, we had to bury him right away. Sir John even read from the Good Book and said some nice words over him."

Growing up around Pa and Moses, one of the things I learned was that things are not always as they seem. Something about this wasn't adding up.

"Where was Paul's body found?" I questioned.

Leonard replied, "On the far side of the camp, about ten yards north of where the remuda was grazing. Gerald's who found him. He is pretty rattled. The boys were cousins who grew up together."

"I sure wouldn't mind looking over the ground, back at that camp. What with carrying constables' commissions and all, it is our place to look into this kind of happening," Moses wryly commented.

I nodded in agreement. We needed to check things out for ourselves. But we didn't necessarily need to let anyone else know about our commissions.

Celine came up with a good cover story. "Leonard, there is a good place to camp about a mile farther ahead on the trail. Why don't you lead the brigade there and start setting up for the evening stop? You can tell Sir John we want to go pay our respects at the gravesite. It is the least we could do for the boy."

Leonard nodded. The three of us rode down the back trail. With it being June, the sun was staying up longer every day, and we would still have daylight to survey the camp, especially where the carts had been. Call it my suspicious nature, but I wanted to determine for myself if it had really been a horse that had killed that boy. I know

Moses and Celine had their doubts as well. If there was anything to find, the three of us would find it.

Within half an hour, we were overlooking the campsite. It had been one of the noon time stops and was close to the river. We tied our horses to some small trees just north of the camp, close to the boy's grave.

"I'm thinkin' we can ignore the south side of the camp. We'll spread out and scour the ground between here and where the carts were parked."

Agreeing with me, Moses moved off to my right while Celine made her way left. Weaving slowly towards the cart tracks, we found nothing amiss. Then, just as we were ready to call it quits, Celine called out, "Over here!"

Moses and I hurried over to see what she had found.

Celine pointed to a rock. "Look how it is sitting. All the other rocks are settled down in the ground. This one is laying on top of crushed grass. It was just placed here recently."

I bent down and picked it up. It was heavy and fit well enough in my hand that it could have been used as a weapon. I turned the rock over in my hand. The bottom was covered with blood. Lots of blood!

"Well, that boy wasn't kicked by any horse. He was murdered. And, little lady, looks like you just found the murder weapon," Moses complimented Celine. "Now, to figure out why someone would have killed him."

"My best bet is that he saw someone doing something suspicious," I surmised. "There was a cart parked by the rock. You can see where the tracks sunk in a little."

Celine spoke up. "The Sinclairs always park the carts in the same order in the circle. This was the sixth cart. So when we get back to the camp, we will be able to tell which cart the murder happened beside."

We then walked over to Paul's grave and paid our respects. Celine, with tears in her eyes, said a prayer in French. Moses grimly vowed, "We'll find the bastard that killed you, son."

Mounting up, we made our way back to Sir John's camp. We agreed that we would tell only Leonard about what we had found. At this point, it might be best if the killer figured he had gotten away with murder.

We came back to a saddened and subdued group of people. Even Sir John was quiet and barely nodded to us. People were just going through the motions. Supper was eaten almost in silence, without the usual chatter and camaraderie that had been taking place in earlier meals.

After eating, Celine and I went looking for Leonard and found him out with the horses. Being down a wrangler, someone would have to help Gerald. Hopefully, we could hire another man at Fort Qu'Appelle, someone that either Leonard or Celine could vouch for.

Leonard, checking to make sure no one else was within earshot, approached us, quietly asking, "Find anything in the sign around the camp?"

I replied, "Paul was murdered, without a doubt."

Leonard bowed his head. "I didn't think that Paul would have been kicked by a horse like that. How was he killed?"

"With a rock, roughly the same size as a horse's hoof. Celine found it beside the sixth cart."

Leonard's eyes opened wide. "That is the cart with a lot of the ladies' cooking supplies. Flour, sugar, canned goods, dried meat, and pemmican."

Celine, in a horrified whisper, gasped, "What if the food was sabotaged?"

In a grave tone, I answered, "We will have to check out the cart as soon as possible. Hopefully, no one gets sick from tonight's meal."

Celine volunteered, "I am the smallest of us, so I can slip into the cart. But I will need some sort of a distraction so that I won't be noticed."

I smiled. "I can cover that. Leonard, can you and the Sinclairs make sure all the stock is hobbled for the night? You can tell them that we saw cat tracks when we were out scouting today."

Celine and I went to our tent to fill Moses in on the plan.

Moses's eyes lit up. "You want me to make a lion's scream later tonight?"

"Yep! A couple of times, enough to get everyone's attention. Be far enough out from the camp that no one will venture out looking for you.. I mean the lion. We don't need Sir John taking potshots at you with his trade musket." I added, "We need to give Celine enough time to check out that cart. She'll be on the first watch tonight. When it's around time for the second watch, let loose. I'll be in the shadows, keeping an eye on the camp and covering Celine's back."

"Gotcha." Moses grinned.

People turned in early that night. The death of the young wrangler had created an atmosphere of despondency. I reckon it was just one of those times when people had had enough for one day.

Two hours later, there came a screaming from out on the prairie! It sounded like a woman wailing in agony. Watching the camp, I saw people flying out of their tents and looking to the southwest, in the direction of the sound. Out of the corner of my eye, I spotted Celine climbing into the supply cart. No one appeared to notice her.

Yet another scream reverberated across the prairie. I made my way over to Sir John, who was peering nervously into the night, his trade musket raised to his shoulder.

"I say—what on earth is happening? Is someone being killed out there?" he apprehensively asked.

Another scream came out of the darkness. Before answering, I chanced a quick glance over to the cart and was relieved to see Celine climbing out.

I turned back to Sir John. "It's the scream of a mountain lion. There ain't many out here, but there can be the odd one. You could fire your musket in the air if you want. Between the sound of the shot and the smell of the burnt powder, the cat will likely just leave the area."

"Jolly good," answered Sir John. Pointing his gun to the sky, he fired it. A sheet of flame shot out the muzzle, accompanied by a thunderous blast. If anyone was still sleepy, they were wide awake now.

"He'll be heading for 'parts unknown' now. You put the run on him, Sir John." Then, turning to the onlookers, I announced, "You can head back to your tents and get some sleep. Sir John has sent that mountain lion packing."

Fifteen minutes later, Celine and I met Moses out by the horses. At least they were settling back down.

Moses dryly commented, "That big cat must've run off after that gunshot. Hell, it even scared me." Then, eyeing Celine, he asked, "How's the grub cart?"

"Could be worse. I think our saboteur was discovered before he could do much. I found this small dark bottle. Could it be poison?"

Moses snatched it out of her hands then gave it a little shake. "It's still full. I'd better be the one to open it. If it's what I think it is, it'll kill ya, graveyard dead, in about as painful a way as you can imagine."

Holding the bottle as far away as possible, Moses slowly worked out the cork, then delicately sniffed the air. He tipped the bottle gently until a minute amount of white crystalline powder dribbled on the ground.

He shook his head. "Yep, that's what I thought when I saw the bottle. It's strychnine, a deadly poison. I met a wolfer one time. A low form of humanity in my books. They use strychnine to poison wolves and other predators for fur. They also use it to control rats and mice from eating the grain. That's bad news because a lot of other animals, like hawks and eagles, die from secondary poisoning. There's enough in this little bottle to kill the whole camp."

"Could he have already put some in an open bag of sugar or flour?" I speculated.

Celine answered. "No, this was in the supply cart. All the bags are still sewn shut. The open bags are in the cooking cart with the pemmican, bacon, and the cooking pots."

I thought for a moment, then suggested a plan. "Let's go outside the camp a ways and dig a hole to bury the powder. Then, we can rinse the bottle out, fill it with dry dirt, and replace the cork. Celine can slip it back into the supply cart where she found it.

"In the morning, Moses and me will do the scouting. Celine, you stay with the camp. You can say that you are going to help Gerald with the horses, but always keep an eye on the carts. If we are right and our killer was interrupted by Paul, there's a good chance he'll want to recover his bottle. He won't know it's been tampered with until he opens it.

"I'll have Sir John ride out with me. Then I can let him know what we've found. I feel pretty confident that he wouldn't sabotage his own expedition. And he just doesn't strike me as a murderer. It's a chance we'll have to take."

Moses remarked, "I'll cover the centre of the trail and keep an eye north as well. I'll come back in early in case there is any trouble."

I nodded. "Good idea. And Moses, can you fill Leonard in on what's going down tomorrow?"

Moses and Celine agreed that this seemed the best course of action. After disposing of the strychnine and refilling the bottle with dirt, Moses and I kept watch to make sure no one was around while Celine quietly made her way back to the supply cart. As she walked by it, she slipped her hand under the canvas and, in a matter of seconds, had tucked the bottle back where she had found it.

While Moses and Celine went to the tent to catch a few winks, I stayed up and kept watch, paying particular attention to the supply cart. Fortunately, no one went near it, and the rest of the night passed without incident.

Come morning, as the camp was having breakfast, I managed to get Sir John's attention. Taking him aside, I murmured, "Once you are done eating, get your horse ready to ride. You have to come scouting with me today. I'll tell you why when we are on our own. It's serious."

I will say this about Sir John, he didn't question me or raise any kind of ruckus. Nodding his head, he just went back to his breakfast.

In forty-five minutes, the camp was struck, and the carts were screeching their way towards Qu'Appelle. I could see that my wife had things in hand with the spare horses and was able to watch the supply cart. Moses was already ahead farther up the trail, scouting.

Sir John was quiet until we were a half mile or so from the carts. As he rode up abreast of me, I started to speak. "In my pocket, I have a constable's commission from Governor MacTavish, as does my grandfather. We are your scouts, but we are also the governor's arm of the law out here. Paul's death seemed suspicious to us—he had spent his life around horses, and it didn't make sense to us that a horse would have caught him off guard like that, kicking him hard enough to kill him. So we went back to the noon campsite and looked for sign. Celine found the rock that was used to kill the lad."

Sir John exhaled sharply. "Murdered? In the camp? Why?"

I explained to him, "Paul was in the wrong place at the wrong time. As best as we can figure by looking at the cart tracks, Paul came across someone attempting to poison the sugar or flour in the supply cart. The 'cougar screaming' last night was actually Moses creating a distraction so that we could check out that cart. Celine found a bottle of strychnine. Fortunately, unopened. I'm thinking that in the process of killing Paul and carrying his body to the far side of the horse herd, the killer didn't have time to get back and retrieve the bottle."

"Bloody hell!" Sir John burst out. "I'll hang the scurvy dog myself! Do you have any idea who?"

"We might know by the time we stop for our midday break. Last night, Moses emptied the bottle and buried the contents, then refilled it with dirt. Celine slipped the bottle back into the cart. Celine stayed with the cavalcade this morning to keep an eye on the cart. I'd lay good odds someone will try to recover the bottle. If she sees anyone snooping around, we have our suspect."

Sir John looked out across the prairie, then solemnly spoke. "You think it's one of my men, don't you?"

"More than likely," I replied. "The Sinclairs have been in business for over twenty years. They've built up a good name. Leonard is Celine's cousin and has helped us before. I'm reasonably confident that young Gerald isn't the killer either. And I don't think it's likely that you would poison your own people."

Sir John anxiously asked, "What can I do?"

"Nothing right now. Just go along with whatever me or my people do."

Sir John pondered a minute. "I hope your plan works. If we have a killer on the loose in our midst, I feel that I would have no choice but to end this expedition."

We rode on in silence for the rest of the morning until arriving at the noon campsite just before the carts. Leonard was already waiting. Nodding at Sir John, he asked me, "He knows?"

I replied, "Yup, I told him everything. Even our plan to flush out the killer."

Celine rode up to us. Speaking in a low whisper, she murmured, "It was Jonesy Harris. He was quick. He rode up to the cart, reached in, and grabbed the bottle. I almost missed seeing it; he was that fast."

Then the carts arrived, and preparations began for the noon time meal. Once the horses were unsaddled and the oxen picketed out to graze, I made my move. Moseying around the camp, jawing with the men as I passed each one in turn, I made my way beside Harris. I then gave a kick and flipped his feet out from under him. As he hit the ground, I drew my pistol. He came up almighty quick but stopped dead still when he heard the *click* as I thumbed back the hammer.

Looking him in the eye, I observed, "Think long and hard on your next move. Now, reach in your pocket, nice and slow. And show everyone your little bottle."

"I don't have any bottle in my…"

There was another ominous *click* behind Harris.

I shook my head. "Now you've gone and done it—you've got my grandfather riled up. At least it looks like he just wants to shoot ya. The last feller to upset him…he scalped alive! Was a horrible sight. So I'm asking you for the last time—hand over that bottle."

Knowing he was bested, he reached into his pocket. He took out the bottle but then rapidly pulled out the cork and threw the bottle at me, snarling, "You can have it."

I just smiled as the bottle bounced off my chest, dry brown dirt flowing out of it. "You don't really think we'd let you have a full bottle of strychnine back, do you?"

I addressed the camp, speaking loudly enough to be heard by all. "This man tried to poison us with strychnine," I declared. "And he murdered young horse herder Paul, when Paul caught him in the act, by bashing him in the head with a rock. We found the rock with fresh blood on it when we went back to Paul's grave."

Sir John came up and stood beside me, glaring at Harris and demanding, "One bloody question. Why?"

Harris stared back at Sir John in sullen silence.

"It might be in your best interest to talk," I suggested. "Your only chance of living a few more days is to talk.

If you think we're gonna haul you all the way back to Fort Garry for a trial, think again. I'm a constable and a representative of the governor. We can have a quick trial at Fort Qu'Appelle and hang you all legal like. Of course, you'd have to make it to Qu'Appelle alive for that to happen. You see those Metis cart drivers over there?" I pointed to Leonard and the Sinclairs. "You murdered one of their people. And I can't be watching over you all the time. See what I'm saying?"

Harris's face suddenly changed. Like a coiled spring being released, he lunged towards Sir John. I saw a tiny flash of shiny steel. By instinct, I squeezed my trigger, firing. Then cocked the hammer, firing again. It happened so quick that I didn't hear Moses shooting as well.

Sir John reacted surprisingly fast, stepping back so quickly that the small dagger only cut through his shirt. Harris's body flinched every time a bullet hit him, but somehow he was still upright on his feet. I fired again, as did Moses. Sir John continued to back away as the killer slowly collapsed to the ground. Harris was dead.

I looked over at Sir John to see if he was hurt. With a wave of his hand, he assured me he was fine.

For the second day in a row there was a grave dug at the noon break. But no one cried at this one. And it may have been a little shallower. We had ground to cover and miles to make.

No one in the camp could make any sense of the events of the last two days. When I questioned Sir John, he claimed to have no idea. Why would Harris try to poison us? We could have all been killed! Something was very wrong here. And we couldn't figure out what. Yet.

When Moses, Celine, and myself were finally alone in our tent that night, we talked over the situation.

"That was cuttin' it almighty close, Jim. Maybe next time we shoot first, then ask questions," Moses wryly remarked with a hint of a grin.

Celine touched my arm. "I thought he was going for you, my husband. In the future, you must be more careful!"

I had to agree with them; that had been a close one. But what was it all really about? Why did Harris try to knife Sir John?

Despite all of the unanswered questions, we still managed to get some much-needed sleep. Leonard and the Sinclairs shared watch rotations with some of Sir John's men.

The next morning, our whole camp was still subdued. But the ladies improved morale with a breakfast of bacon and pancakes, washed down with some eastern maple syrup. With a decent start on the trail and the stock performing well, we rolled into Fort Qu'Appelle a little after two in the afternoon.

Chapter Seven

Sir John, Moses, Celine, and myself made our way to the general store. Being in luck, we found the chief trader, a wiry, grey-haired Scotsman named Clyde Buchanan.

"What can I do for you folks? Come to do a bit of trading, eh?" Looking out the window, he observed the carts. "Ah, I recognize the Sinclairs. You're that expedition that MacTavish mentioned in our last dispatches."

"We are indeed, my good man. I'm Sir John Jacob Augustus Martindale the Third, the leader of this expedition," Sir John heartily boomed. "These are my scouts—Moses Munro, his grandson Jim, and Jim's wife, Celine."

The old trader glanced over at me while Sir John was introducing himself. His eyes gave a slight roll, but he kept his composure. Probably didn't have many Sirs with four names pass through these parts.

After a round of handshakes, Sir John gave the trader a list of supplies we would be needing. More flour, sugar, and canned goods for the cooks. Also a rough axle to replace the sabotaged one that Leonard had patched on the trail. The Sinclairs would hand carve the axle to fit their cart.

Once Sir John left to oversee the supplies being loaded, we could talk to the trader in private. Showing him our commissions, I explained, "In addition to scouting for Sir John's expedition, Governor MacTavish has asked us to look into the rumours of someone trying to stir up trouble between the tribal Indians. Sounds like someone is looking to get a war going. What have you been hearing from your dealings with the tribes?"

Buchanan's face darkened as he nodded. "I'm afraid it's more than rumours. There are shootings happening and attacks on Indian camps. Some have been wounded and horses and supplies stolen. And sadly, a few have been killed. The strange thing is, no one can say what tribe is doing the raiding. It's to the point the Assiniboine blame the Saulteaux, who are blaming the Cree, and everyone is also pointing fingers at the Blackfoot. I could understand the tribes of the Iron Confederacy blaming the Blackfoot but not each other. The Plains Cree, Assiniboine, Saulteaux, and the Metis have been living in peace with each other for generations."

Moses spoke up. "Who gains anything from an all-out war between the tribes?"

"No one," answered Buchanan. "It would be disastrous for all involved. And would likely even bankrupt the Bay."

"We'll just have to keep digging then," I thoughtfully replied. "If it does get any worse, we're supposed to escort Sir John back to Fort Garry as soon as possible. There is something fishy going on with this expedition as well."

I then proceeded to tell Buchanan about the sabotaged axle, the attempted poisoning, and the murder of young Paul. "We figured out who the killer was. A man named Jonesy Harris, one of Sir John's men. We had to shoot him before he could stick a knife into the boss man. I just can't see how dinosaur bones are worth killing over. There is something more going on here. But Sir John seems to be oblivious."

I asked the trader for some writing material. And then wrote a report on the events that had occurred thus far on this expedition, addressing it to Governor MacTavish. It could go to Fort Garry with the next rider or cart brigade heading east.

After saying our goodbyes to Buchanan, we moseyed around the fort. Other than Fort Garry, all the other Hudson Bay posts were built out of logs. This one was still fairly new, being built just three years earlier. There were warehouses for storage of furs and trade goods, as well as stables and a blacksmith shop. There were living quarters, offices, and a kitchen. This place was a going concern, whose main concern was the fur trading business.

Leonard and the Sinclair men had managed to replace the axle by now and were almost finished reloading the cart with the heavy boxes of digging tools.

Leonard motioned to us, and we made our way towards him. "We will be ready in a few minutes. I found a fella, an old Iroquois called Milton. I've worked with him before, and he's steady. Sir John has hired him on as another horse herder."

"Good." Moses nodded. "That will help out a lot. I'm betting he was out in the Rockies years ago. He'll be able to take some shifts on night watch. We might have to scout a day or two ahead, depending on water. Farther west, we'll be out in front lookin' for problems. He'll be someone you can rely on when we're not around."

We travelled four miles before making camp for the night. After our evening meal, Celine and Leonard commenced to outline our route to Sir John.

Leonard began, "We'll follow the Forks cart trail for roughly six days. Maybe less if we make good time. Then, we leave the trail and head north until we make contact with the South Saskatchewan River. That should take a day, more or less. We follow the river until we find a reasonable way down into the valley. We set up a base camp, and people can spread out in groups of two or three, searching for dinosaur bones."

Sir John spoke up. "I've been told that the river valley is more eroded farther west. The sandstone is softer than the fossilized bones, which are actually rock. The more erosion, the greater the likelihood of finding exposed fossils. I say we go farther up the river valley to the forks of the Red Deer River right off the bat."

Celine, managing not to blow up at him, answered, "The closer we get to the Forks, the greater the chances are of an encounter with the Blackfoot. You do not want to run into them. They still consider the Forks part of their territory. As do the Cree and the Assiniboine."

Celine continued, "We have some friends amoung the Assiniboine, at least one small band. Hopefully, by now, the Cree have all heard about the trade goods offered by the governor for our safe passage.

"There are no deals with the Blackfoot, anywhere. There are no Hudson Bay posts in Blackfoot territory. They travel to the Bay forts to trade. The message is very simple: STAY OUT OF BLACKFOOT TERRITORY!"

She concluded, "Once the expedition is settled in a camp close to the South Saskatchewan River, Jim, Moses, and myself will go scouting for a few days up on the prairie. If we see no buffalo herds or Indians, you might be able to move farther west."

Duncan Alexander nodded. "Yes, I see now. If there's no buffalo herds, there's no tribes hunting."

Moses lifted an eyebrow at Alexander but said nothing. I was thinking the same thing. This feller's not just here to dig. But what is he here for? He was the oldest man here, after Moses and Milton. Sir John did seem to rely on him.

Everyone soon turned in for an uneventful night.

For the next six days, we made good time. Cart trails, as a rule, followed a route where there were reasonably reliable sources of water and the easiest pulling—not necessarily the straightest, but in the long run, the quickest.

On the seventh day, we arrived at the South Saskatchewan River valley. After searching for an hour, we found a passable slope that the carts could use to safely descend to the valley floor.

After Celine warned everyone to keep an eye out for rattlesnakes, a camp was set up. The carts were placed in a defensive perimeter around the tents. The stock was allowed to graze under the watchful eye of the herders.

Taking Sir John aside, the three of us laid out our plan, with Celine starting. "We are roughly two days from the Forks, closer to five with the carts. Being in an area that three tribes call theirs, it can be a dangerous place. Some trade takes place, but no white man can stay for long. We will go back up to the prairie and scout in a circle to the south and west. When we get to the South Saskatchewan west of the Forks, we will follow it downstream back towards camp. If we don't see any sign of the Blackfoot, we will move the expedition a little farther west."

Moses then spoke up. "I just want to make sure you understand—MacTavish was very clear in his orders to us. At the first sign of any trouble with the tribes, we are to escort you back to the closest fort."

Sir John's face fell a little. "I understand. But surely, if there aren't any buffalo or Indians around…" His voice trailed off.

"We can hope," I muttered. "But until we have a gander out west, you will stay right here. There are eroded places along this valley where you can start searching for bones."

Finishing with Sir John, we then looked for Leonard and old Milton and found them with the stock. We let them know where we intended to scout and that we might be gone for a few days. We knew we could leave the expedition in the care of these two. With the addition of Milton, there were enough experienced men to handle the night watch without us. We turned in early for the night, as we were planning to be at the rim of the river valley come daybreak. Hopefully, Sir John's optimism would be justified.

CHAPTER EIGHT

Standing beside our mounts, just below the valley's rim, the three of us watched the light spreading as the sun rose in the sky. To the north, out on the plain, was grass. Just grass, for miles and miles. Prairie fires kept the brush and trees to a minimum. Below us on the grassy floodplain, the rest of our expedition was starting to awaken.

Taking my time and scanning the valley with Pa's field glasses for several minutes, I determined that there were no Indian camps in the vicinity. With the only trees being some cottonwoods growing close to the river and very little brush anywhere, a circle of teepees would have stood out.

Moses broke the silence. "Looks like it's time to have a look around on our side of the river."

Leading our horses up out of the valley and onto the prairie, I once again carefully scanned the horizon with the glasses. Nothing. It was time to get riding and earn our wages.

We rode southwest across the dry prairie grass towards a range of hills. Celine knew of a spring where we could water the horses and make camp for the night. If we were lucky, no one would be there. The Blackfoot claimed both sides of the South Saskatchewan. And with it starting to get harder to find enough buffalo to feed their people, there was a good chance we might run into them even farther east on our side of the river.

After reaching the hills in the early afternoon, Celine led us to the spring. It was a small pond formed by a seep on the north side and base of a hill. Carefully approaching, we found ourselves alone at the water. We were lucky, as the ground showed the tracks of at least twenty-five unshod horses. No travois marks or any sign of women and children. Hunting party or war party? Assiniboine or Blackfoot?

Moses swung down off his horse for a closer look. "One of these warriors is wearing boots. Definitely something to keep in mind. Looks like they watered here and moved on."

"There are other springs out here," commented Celine. "And it's only a day to the Bad River."

That's what the Indians call the South Saskatchewan south and west of the Forks?" I asked.

"Yes," she answered. "When we reach it, you'll see why. The walls of the river valley are steep and barren."

"Let's boil some water for us and let the horses drink. Then we can be figgerin' what we need to do," uttered Moses.

Later, as I was filling my tin cup with tea, I said, "We need to determine which way those pony tracks are heading. If they lead off in an easterly direction, we'd better get back to the carts. South or west, we can probably keep scouting. If they are travelling west, we'll have to angle off, so we don't make contact if we can help it."

I looked to Celine. "If they're travelling south, can we turn west and find water?"

Celine cautiously answered me. "There are springs. It's getting on in the afternoon. Our horses are good for water now, so if we made a dry camp, it wouldn't be serious. We could easily make the river sometime tomorrow morning."

Moses weighed in. "Sounds like a good idea to me. If we're lucky, these Indians headed south, maybe for the Cypress Hills. If we ain't lucky, we angle northwest to the river, water the horses again, and get back to Sir John."

Not wanting to waste any more time, we mounted up. After following the tracks southwest for almost an hour, we broke off the trail and rode northwest towards the river. The sun was setting when we stopped to make camp. Not wanting to take the chance of being seen, we hobbled the horses in a low spot surrounded by low hills. There would be no hot meal or tea tonight. Just water that had been boiled earlier from our canteens and some pemmican.

Having spent a night with no disturbances, we were reasonably well-rested come morning. As the sun was just starting to rise, the three of us climbed the tallest hill. Close to the crest, we dropped on our hands and knees and crawled to the top, then carefully looked out in all four directions. We were in luck! No buffalo, no Indians.

In less than twenty minutes, we were mounted and carefully meandering to the river, below the summits of the hills. Every half hour or so, one of us would crawl up a hill for a good look around. We didn't use Pa's field glasses for this, either. No way we could chance on any glare off them giving us away.

Midday found us overlooking the South Saskatchewan. No wonder the Natives and Celine's people called it the

Bad River. From where we were standing, it looked more like a deep gorge than a valley, barren steep walls with ancient arroyos running from top to bottom.

"Looks like if we pick out one of the more manageable arroyos, we could ride down to the river," surmised Moses.

It only took a few minutes to find an accessible route that descended to the river. It was steep in places, but our sure-footed horses got us to the water without mishap. After our mounts had drank their fill, we hobbled them while we made our dinner. Finding plenty of dry wood amongst some cottonwoods, we boiled water. Soon, we were washing down more of our pemmican with hot tea.

"Can we ride for the rest of the day along the river?" I asked Celine.

"I'm not sure on that. We had never travelled along this river with our carts. I know some of our hunters watered horses here. Other than that, I can't say," she answered.

"I don't think we want to spend too much time down here anyway," voiced Moses. "Too easy to get trapped. I'm a thinkin' our best bet is to stay here till almost sundown. The horses can graze, and we can water them again before we go back up to the prairie. We could find a good spot close to the top, spend the night, and head east towards the cavalcade in the morning. Between someone sabotaging the cart axle, finding strychnine, young Paul being murdered, and Sir John almost being knifed, I think we'd best be getting back to Leonard and the expedition."

This seemed like a sound idea. And Lord knows the horses could use the extra graze and a bit of a rest. It would be a good time for us to clean up and wash the sweat out of our clothes. Moses kept watch on the horses while Celine and I washed, enjoying our little break together.

Three hours later, we mounted up. Taking our time so as not to tire out our horses on the steep climb, we picked our way up to the rim. Finding a decent-sized swale about fifty yards across, we stopped and set up camp. Here, we hobbled the horses and unrolled our bedrolls. Celine, as per usual, took first watch, I took second, and Moses took the last shift.

Celine climbed into her bedroll as I began my shift. I walked up the few yards to the rim and stood listening to the night sounds. In the distance, a coyote howled up the river to the southwest. A couple more joined in, also upstream. Other than the coyotes, it was quiet… too quiet!

Moving silently, I made my way back to Celine and Moses. Waking them as quietly as possible, I whispered, "Saddle up, we don't have much time. It's way too quiet downriver. We've gotta get some miles behind us, now!"

Instantly alert, they wasted no time asking questions. We were skedaddling out of there in as little time as it takes to saddle up. For the first two miles, we made a steady pace. It was a fine line between how fast we could travel without pushing the horses too hard. We kept travelling eastwards, slowing to a walk every half hour and stopping to listen.

The sun was just starting to rise when we stopped for a break and to check our back trail. Looking west through Pa's field glasses, I could see dust. And then could make out buckskin-clad riders on our trail. We needed to get makin' tracks!

They had likely been camped downriver from us. One of their scouts must have found us and went back to get help from the others. I suspect they planned to hit us just as the sun started to rise. We were already gone, but our tracks were easy to follow.

The sun was climbing higher over the dry landscape. By now, we were east of the Forks, with the South Saskatchewan River to the north of us. Our situation was going from bad to worse. Now, there were more riders aiming to cut us off from the river. We had to angle southeast, out towards the sand hills. We had no choice; we had to push our horses to their limit. The only thing going for us was that our pursuers' horses had to be playing out as well. Could ours outlast theirs? Iffy. We were going to need a place to hole up, and soon.

It was then that we came across the buffalo waller with the chokecherry trees. And it was here we had made our stand.

The South Saskatchewan River Valley (known as the 'Bad River' by the Natives)

Photo by Del Pratt

CHAPTER NINE

LATE AFTERNOON, JUNE 15, 1867

I had learned a lot from my grandfather in my short twenty years. Having lived in the Rockies for years back in the 1820s and still having his hair, he had a lot to teach. And now, with my wife who was raised on the prairie, the three of us made a good team. We could all size up a situation and count on each other to act. Looking back, I'm pretty sure that's why we survived the events of the afternoon. Even though Moses was wounded, he could ride. All in all, we had come out of that fight in decent shape and had killed nine of the sixteen men who had attacked us.

We continued riding northeast, back towards Sir John's camp. I finally broke the silence. "Anyone think we're gonna get out of this without another fight?"

"Non!" answered Celine. "They'll be back. And maybe even have more men with them."

"I'm afeared she is right," agreed Moses. "I have no idea who they are. Why would white men be dressed as Indians?

"We gotta do some figgerin' on how we get outta this mess. If'n I was the boss man of that outfit, I would herd us into the hills. Then take my time, surround us, and let the heat finish us off."

I pondered for a moment. "Could we angle sharp to the north and hit the South Saskatchewan east of the forks? Even if they left scouts watching the river, our odds would be better than out here. We need water, and if they have men posted at the closest springs, we're done."

Celine nodded. "Oui, I think that's our best bet." Then, looking to Moses, she asked, "How is the arm?"

"It's fine. A little stiff, but it'll hold a carbine when we need it to. How far you reckon to the South Saskatchewan?"

"Maybe three hours," answered Celine. "Provided we don't have company."

"I'm thinkin' we'll have company alright," growled Moses. "That was a young bunch, maybe a scouting party. I'm a thinkin' our troublemakers out here must have more men and an older, experienced leader. Veteran fighters, red or white, would have finished us off on the first charge."

The conversation died down as we were getting thirsty but daren't touch our canteens yet. The heat didn't die down, though. If anything, it got hotter and drier as the afternoon wore on.

The horses' heads were starting to droop by the time we were finally able to see the river. I carefully scanned the valley with the field glasses but saw no one. We cautiously made our way down to the water. Once we got close, there was no holding back the horses. They were gonna have a drink, come hell or high water. They had earned it; they had done their part in saving our hides.

After the horses had drank their fill, we walked them downriver until we came to some cottonwoods.

"We can rest here until dark. But I think we should cover as much ground as we can tonight." I continued with my opinion, "As the sun is setting, we'll start going east along the river. This valley is considerably wider than the Bad River. I'm figuring we don't have to go to the top right away. I could slip up there towards morning and look the country over."

"What if we get attacked in the valley? We have one direction we cannot run to," Celine responded as she pointed at the water flowing by us.

"It is at that," spoke up Moses, "but it's also one side they won't attack us from. If we get hit, we can fort up by the river."

"That would mean shooting the horses and using their bodies as cover," I said in a low voice.

Moses solemnly stated, "It would, Jim. But it would give us a chance."

I could tell the idea didn't appeal to him either. However, there are times when drastic action has to be taken. I was just hoping that this wasn't one of them.

As darkness approached, we saddled up and commenced with our journey. There was no talking now, just listening. We didn't know for sure if anyone was in the valley hunting for us, but then again, we had no way of knowing if they weren't. Our ears were attuned to the sounds of the night—the ripple of the water, the croak of a frog, the distant howling of coyotes. An attacker would be as quiet as possible, but hopefully, we would have some warning. Also, seein' that even as the sun went down, it was staying hot, we had to be alert for the warning rattle of snakes. They would be out hunting mice and ground squirrels. Most would hear us coming and move out of the way, trying to avoid us. Again, hopefully!

In silence, we made our way east along the river. For the most part, we were riding in grass with some scrub brush. Prairie fires kept the brush from getting too thick. Here and there were the blackened remains of smaller trees. Even so, some cottonwoods still managed to grow along the river.

With no moon, we had only the faint glow on the north-western horizon for light. Having a light breeze from the southwest was like the old good-news, bad-news scenario. We could hear anyone coming up behind us, but anyone ahead would hear us.

Two hours after we set out, we came to the spot where the river made a loop, almost meeting itself. Here, the walls of the valley were closer to the river. The ancient washes that carved their way into the walls of the valley made perfect cover to set an ambush.

I was riding out front at this time. I raised my arm, and Celine and Moses held their horses up alongside me.

"I don't like this," I whispered. "If'n I was gonna bushwhack somebody riding along the river, it would be just ahead as we went around that bend, close to the valley walls. Notice there is no place to ride up topside from there either."

Moses agreed. "I don't like the head-on approach either."

"We could go back a couple hundred yards," Celine suggested. "Our horses might make it up that arroyo."

"That could work. We can't go ahead without risking an ambush. And staying here isn't getting us closer to the carts," I answered. Moses nodded in the darkness.

We turned our horses around, and Celine took the lead. In an hour, we had climbed our way to the rim of the river valley. Dismounting to give our horses a rest, I handed my reins to Celine and walked down our backtrail for about a hundred yards.

Drawing my Leech and Rigdon, I waited in the darkness, kneeling close to the arroyo's edge. All was quiet. Maybe we were wrong? Were we actually ahead of our adversaries? Or did we whip them bad enough that no one was coming after us?

Suddenly, I caught a whiff, a different smell. Sweat! Then, a slight scraping sound.

I drew the hammer back and let'er rip, firing three shots in the direction of the sound as I rolled.

There were two loud blasts and blazes of flame, and I heard the thud of bullets hitting the ground, right where I had just been. After firing the last two rounds from my pistol towards the flashes, I heard a light thump, then a cry of pain. Holstering the Rigdon and pulling out my Green River, I waited. Nothing. Then I heard someone crawling away. There was silence. I waited for a good ten minutes before cautiously making my way back to Celine and Moses. When I got within earshot, I whispered, "It's me, Jim."

Celine threw her arms around me, tears in her eyes. "Mon cheri, tu es en vie!"

"Easy, girl, you're squeezing hard enough to break a rib."

"All I could do to keep her up here," growled Moses. "Told her the last shots were yours. If you needed us, you'd call out. Good thing you got here when you did, though. Even I was starting to worry."

"We better get makin' some tracks. It sounded like there were two of them; I hit one." I added, "But who knows if there are more slinkin' around here."

Mounting up, we rode east at a trot, trying to conserve our horses. When we made it back to the expedition, they'd have to be rested for a few days for sure.

The sun was slowly peeking over the horizon when we stopped for a short break and to listen. I scanned our back trail with Pa's field glasses. Nothing caught my eye, but the light was still poor. In another half hour, I would check again. We would have to get back to the river soon. In this heat, the horses would be needing water again.

"We can't be more than ten miles from the camp," estimated Celine. "We'll go five more and make our way to the river. After watering and resting the horses, we'll push on to the carts."

"No arguin' here," declared Moses.

"Me neither." I nodded. "Let's hit the trail."

By the time another five miles was behind us, the horses were tiring. This time, we found an easier path from the prairie down to the valley floor. It was getting hotter as the day progressed. The grass was so dry it was crunching under our horses' feet. Most of it was still last year's grass, as there was very little new growth.

After watering the horses, we hobbled them for a short graze. Moses and Celine caught a few winks in the shade of some young cottonwoods while I kept watch. So far, so good. But we weren't home free yet. It could be a long five miles ahead of us. After that last shootin' scrape, it was a pretty safe bet that someone would be after us. How many, though?

Looking at the tallest of the cottonwoods, I had the idea to climb it a ways and have a look with the glasses.

I worked my way up as far as I dared, trying not to break any branches (and possibly a leg if I fell with the branch.) I searched the river valley behind us and saw nothing. Taking time to scan up towards the rim, I saw no one. What was over the top out on the prairie, I had no idea. I raised the glasses to take one last look up the valley and froze. There was dust! Too far away to tell how many riders but at least as many as the last time we socialized!

After rapidly scrambling down from the tree, I woke the pair up from their nap. "We gotta move. Now! Riders coming. Two miles, maybe a little more, but they're not wasting any time."

We hightailed outta there, headin' east along the river.

Moses yelled to Celine and me, "If they get too close, I'll drop off and hold 'em back! You two keep goin'. No back talk, neither. I mean it!"

I shook my head. "Not gonna happen. They'd still get us. We'll find a place with some cover. The gunfire might bring some help!"

We kept up a steady pace for twenty minutes, our enemies getting ever closer. It was bad enough being hunted, but not knowing by who was even worse. We had to be within two miles of Sir John. He didn't strike me as a fighter, but something in the back of my mind was telling me his men just might be. The Metis would be ready if we could warn them.

"Time to see what these horses have left in them," I called out. We broke into a gallop, and for a minute, it looked like we were gaining ground. I pulled my pistol and fired a shot towards our pursuers.

"You can't hit anything from here," cried out Celine.

"I know. But gunfire might alert the camp," I shouted back. Turning in the saddle, I could see they were closing in on us. Our horses were spent. With no choice, we ducked into a small grove of willows growing along the river. Tying the horses on the river's edge, we found cover and waited. We reloaded the empty chambers on our pistols. I then focused the field glasses on the approaching riders. Like the previous attackers, most of them were dressed in buckskin. But again, some had the beards of white men.

This time, there was no charge at us. A man with a grey beard appeared to be giving orders. Whoever he was, he was a whole lot more organized and cautious. He had the men dismount well out of range of our carbines. Then, on his command, they split into two skirmish lines of ten to twelve men each. The leader stayed back, remaining mounted, as the men started advancing on us.

Once within range, they dropped down into the grass. One bunch started to sporadically fire at us while the other advanced. Then the rear line advanced while the front fired at us. We were in serious trouble!

I yelled to Celine, "The next time they drop down, you jump in that river and swim away as fast as you can."

"Non, I am needed here!" she retorted.

"I wasn't asking," I barked.

"I don't take orders!" she snapped.

When the next line rose to advance, we fired a couple rounds, then ducked down as musket balls came flying in and shredded a few willow branches. Black powder smoke was hanging in the air, thick enough that we could feel it burning in our eyes. The roar of the guns firing was deafening. Some of our shots were hitting home, but not enough. I gave us another ten minutes at best. Even though their skirmish lines were thinning, they kept coming at us. I saw movement through the smoke and fired, hearing the satisfying thump of a bullet hitting home.

Then I heard it—the shrill whistle of a Whitworth sniper rifle! Leonard was here! Help had arrived.

The rolling thunder of .58 calibre rifle muskets followed. I was quite familiar with the sound of these guns, after encountering them when rescuing my sister two years ago. Only now, the volleys were coming from those rifles about every six or seven seconds.

Our saviours had the high ground and could see the skirmishers in the grass. Two more volleys and the attackers lost interest in us and ran like hell back to their horses. A few more fell, but a good fifteen made it to their horses and fled up the river valley.

"Anyone hit?" I anxiously demanded.

"Good here," coughed Moses. "Just got a whiff of smoke."

"Celine?" I called out. When there was no answer, I looked frantically to my right and saw her lying on the ground, blood in her hair. My heart dropped, and I raced over to her. No, Lord, not her! Then I saw her chest rise. She was breathing—she was alive! Checking her over thoroughly, I found a small cut on the left side of her head, beside a lump that was already swelling and starting to bruise.

Celine began to stir. "My head hurts," she moaned. She opened her eyes and calmed as she saw me gazing down at her. Then, with a start, she remembered where she was. She struggled to sit up as she worriedly asked, "Are you okay? What about Moses?"

I reassured her and eased her back down. "We are just fine. Especially now that you are back with us. You took a nasty blow to the head, my girl."

By now, Sir John and his men rode up to us. With concern on his face, he inquired, "Is she badly hurt?" He spoke in the crisp tones of a commanding officer, with no trace remaining of the educated English professor.

Surprised, I looked up at him before replying, "She took a nasty bump on the head. I think she'll recover with some rest, but we need to get her back to camp as soon as possible."

"We'll get her there, lad." Turning, he called out, "Sergeant Alexander! Have the lads make a stretcher to transport Mrs. Munro back to the carts."

"Aye, Captain," answered Alexander.

Moses was looking up at Sir John on his horse. Eyeing the rifle in the Englishman's hands, he commented dryly, "Mighty fancy dinosaur digging tools you have there."

Sir John smiled and let out a chuckle. "Brand new Snyder Enfield breech-loading conversions." Climbing down off his horse, he came over and stood by me and Celine. "Madam, I am Captain Jack Swanson of the Coldstream Guards, at your service. We will get you safely back to camp."

He then turned to face me and Moses. "I apologize for the subterfuge and theatrics. I couldn't take the risk of you being captured if you had full knowledge of our true mission. I will fully explain when we get back to camp."

Moses said with a twinkle in his eye, "I may have been born at night, but it wasn't last night. We knew somethin' wasn't on the up and up with you and your crew."

Sir John then addressed me directly. "My men and I will take turns carrying your wife's stretcher. I will start the first shift."

I nodded to Sir John. "Thank you. And I've got the front end."

Chapter Ten

We made it back to camp well before dark. The Sinclair ladies immediately took charge of Celine and laid her down gently in one of the tents. She had collapsed into a deep sleep soon after we started carrying her. I watched as they put cool, damp cloths on her head. Abigail, one of the ladies, shooed me out of the tent, saying, "She'll be fine. Just let her sleep. We have been treating people for years. Don't worry. One of us will come and get you if you are needed."

I left the tent and made my way over to the fire where Captain Jack, as he was now being called, was seated on a camp stool. Moses handed me a cup of steaming hot tea as I sat down. Alexander dished me a bowl of hearty stew, which I tore into ravenously.

With my belly full, I was ready to hear what was actually going on with the expedition.

"As I told you earlier, I'm Captain Jack Swanson, currently on loan to the Foreign Office from the Coldstream Guards. My men are all volunteers from the Guards and veterans of the Crimean War. I had never met Harris before, as he was from the second battalion. I suspect the real Jonesy Harris was killed, and that imposter was put in his place.

"I believe you were already having your suspicions about us. I do apologize for the deception, especially since it was all for naught, as it appears that a spy managed to infiltrate our operation.

"Moses has filled me in on your mission for Governor MacTavish. It appears we are after the same people. It's a long and complicated story.

"You have possibly heard that America is in the process of buying Russian America, called Alyeska by Russia. Our diplomats tell us that not all in the Russian government are happy. However, Czar Alexander has managed to convince his cabinet to go along with this. Sources of our British foreign minister have indicated that the Czar has been wanting to sell Alyeska for some time now. After losing the Crimean War, Russia needs money. The Czar realizes that Alyeska is too far from Saint Petersburg to defend if Britain did try to add it to British North America. Britain was very interested in purchasing it and may have had a chance until we got involved in the debacle of the Crimean War. We joined the French to help the Turks fight Russia. In the end, we did win the war, but there was no way Alexander was going to sell us anything.

"Enter a small group of Russian aristocratic junior army and navy officers. These people are not happy with Russia selling a colony or losing the war ten years ago. They wanted another crack at the Turks. They had plans in place to hold a coup d'etat and replace the Czar with a distant cousin of royal blood. Fortunately, one of our operatives stumbled upon this operation, and the Foreign Office let their counterparts in Russia know."

I was puzzled. "But what does all of that have to do with what's happening out here with us?"

Captain Jack took a swallow of his tea and then continued. "Well, by the time we discovered the conspiracy, the global part of their plan had been launched. They had plans for diversions abroad to keep Britain occupied so we wouldn't get involved. While the Russian government had executed the leaders of the conspiracy, parts of their plans were already in motion. A Hudson Bay turncoat was on his way to Rupert's Land with a group of mercenaries recruited from the Asian Steppes. Their goal was to get a major war started over here between the Indian tribes. That would possibly keep Britain distracted enough not to help the Turks this time around. And if the war spilled across the forty-ninth parallel, it might keep the Americans distracted from buying Alyeska."

"Let me guess," uttered Moses. "That's who we've been fightin' for two days?"

"It is," Jack affirmed.

"Did MacTavish know about this when he hired us?" I questioned Jack.

"He did. But he was sworn to secrecy. We needed the best scouts we could get who were available. And the dinosaur expedition was the most plausible cover story we could come up with. If we can stop a war and keep hundreds or thousands of people from getting killed, it's worth our lives."

"That's why the governor tried to talk Celine into staying at the fort," I surmised. "Not that knowing this would have changed her mind." Looking Jack in the eye, I declared, "No more secrets!"

"You have my word on that, Jim," the captain answered.

"What's the plan now?" inquired Moses. "I'm a thinkin' your renegade has lost a lot of his men. We killed nine in our first fight and must have wounded some. Last night, Jim put a pistol ball in another. How many were killed when your boys opened up on them this afternoon?"

Alexander spoke up. "We found four bodies. And as near as we could tell, there were seven more blood trails. I would think his mercenaries are starting to wonder if they will live long enough to collect their wages. One more engagement on our terms should send any survivors back to Russia."

"Cut the head off the snake," interjected Moses, "and the snake dies. We just have to find the leader and kill him. What do you know about him?"

"Very little, I'm afraid," Captain Jack replied. "It's rumoured he was let go by the Hudson Bay Company many years ago. It was suspected he had committed murder, but it was never proven."

At that time, Isaiah Williams approached us. "Captain, sir, we 'ave all the rifles cleaned." Looking to Moses and me, he offered, "Would you like us to see to your carbines? We'd be 'appy to clean them for you and oil them up as well."

"Go ahead, fellers." Moses grinned. "Way you boys was shootin' this afternoon, I reckon you know your way around a rifle."

"Those breech-loading rifles of yours look new," I commented to Alexander.

"Aye, laddie, they are. In fact, we have them to test and see how well they work. Young Adams managed to get off seven shots in less than a minute. A good accurate rifle, I'd say."

"I'd say they get the job done alright," I agreed.

A shadow passed over the sergeant's face. "We sure could've used them at Inkerman." He sighed.

"Amen to that," voiced the captain.

Moses yawned. "We can do more thinkin' on this in the morning. We need some rest, and I can see Jim is wanting to check in on Celine."

The gathering broke up for the night. Leonard had the night watch in hand, telling us to get a good night's sleep.

I stepped into the tent and looked down at Celine. I was reassured to hear her strong, regular breathing. This was a good sign. I figured she would have one hell of a headache but should pull through okay. I bent down and gently kissed her forehead, not wanting to disturb her.

After fetching and unrolling my bedroll, I settled beside Celine, wanting to be there as soon as she woke up. I had trouble falling asleep. My mind was racing. Celine and I had plans for our future—start a family, maybe build a horse ranch somewhere in this western country. But somehow, our simple guiding job had turned into an international mission to prevent a war from breaking out. And Celine had gotten hurt. Lord, I just want her to wake up and be okay.

There was still no change in Celine when the sun rose. Her breathing remained steady, and that was a good sign. Mary Sinclair entered the tent and put a cold cloth on her head, telling me, "You go eat. There is nothing you can do here. We will let you know if anything changes."

Breakfast was being served, and eating seemed to be a better idea than arguing with Mary. After two cups of tea and some hot bannock with a venison steak, I felt ready for the day.

Meandering through the camp, I took the time to thank each one of the soldiers personally. All were wanting to know how Celine was doing. As Pa would say, we had all seen the elephant together and were becoming a close-knit group.

A circle was gathering: Captain Jack, Moses, Sergeant Alexander, Leonard, Mark Sinclair, and the old Iroquois, Milton.

"How's our girl doing this morning?" Moses asked with a concerned tone in his voice.

"Not much change, but she is breathing stronger. That's got to be a good thing."

"It is, laddie. Just give her some rest and time. I've seen this many times in my twenty-five years in the queen's army." Alexander was trying to alleviate my fears, but I couldn't help but worry. I had never seen her look helpless before. She had always been the one to patch up us Munro men.

Captain Jack briskly asked, "Any ideas, gentlemen? We need to figure out our next course of action. We've hit them hard in the last few days." Looking at me, the captain continued, "Especially you people. With what you left for the vultures and what we added to his casualties, he's lost a lot of men."

"What he's got left might be rethinking their options too," Moses pondered. "Whatever they were drawin' for fightin' wages might seem a little light about now." Then he added, "I don't know anything about the horse people from the steppes of Asia. But I know a lot about horse tribes over on this side of the ocean. One thing is that no tribe can afford to take a lot of casualties. His Asians may be pulling out on him. The white men he has might be more motivated, depending on who they are."

"If they are Russian soldiers, they might stick around, depending how many are left," speculated Alexander.

Leonard spoke up. "Even if the Asians wanted to go home, how would they get there? Without the leader, they have no way home. If the white men are Russian and desert with them, some of them might know how to make their way to the ocean and catch a ship."

"Captain, how did they get here?" I asked.

"Our sources assume they came to the west coast of British Columbia on a Russian ship. They then found guides that could lead them through to the Yellowhead Pass."

Moses remarked, "So unless some of the Asians or the soldiers know their way back, they are stuck here."

A thought crossed my mind. "Captain, you said yesterday this traitor isn't a young man. Why would an older man take on a mission like this? For the money? Revenge at the Bay for being fired?"

Following my train of thought, I looked to Moses and asked, "Would you take on a job halfway around the world just for money? Especially if you had to cross an ocean, keep a bunch of mercenaries in line, and then cross the Rocky Mountains? All to start a war?"

Moses pondered, then shook his head. "Does seem a bit much for an older man, don't it?"

We all fell quiet, trying to puzzle out the reason an old man would take on such a daunting task.

It was Milton the Iroquois who broke the silence with one word. "Gold."

Part Two

The Gold

CHAPTER ELEVEN

"Gold! What are you talking about?" I exclaimed.

Milton answered in a slow, deliberate voice. "My grandfather worked for the Nor'Westers back in the 1790s. He was young then. He had the gift of getting people to talk. People naturally liked him. Even the Blackfoot traded and told him accounts of their history. He told one of the stories to me when I was a boy. It was about some white men who came from the east in a big canoe. They were looking for shiny rocks. They found plenty on a river flowing east and into what we now call the Missouri. The Blackfoot told my grandfather that the strange men had leather bags full of these little rocks." He paused for a minute, trying to remember.

"How long before your grandfather's time did these men come up the river?" Captain Jack inquired.

"It was before the Blackfoot had guns or horses. I remember that part of the story." Milton paused, then continued, "Yes, I remember now how the story went. The Indian camp was upstream from the men who were digging gold out of the river bank.

"Three young girls went looking for berries along the river. They spotted the white men—the first time they had ever seen any—and stayed to watch them. One of the girls slipped on the river bank and cried out. The men ran after the girls, grabbing two and taking them back to their camp. The lone girl made it back to her people and told them what had happened. Some warriors went to go rescue the other two girls from the white men.

"As I remember it, the Blackfoot killed all the white men. But one of the girls and two of their warriors were killed by guns. After the fight, the medicine man wanted the shiny metal returned to the earth as it had brought bad luck. They just buried it again, close to where it had been dug up. After all, they had no use for shiny, soft rocks."

Moses turned to Milton. "So you think this Hudson Bay turncoat we're after found out about that buried gold? Any idea which river they were on?"

"No idea. But when I worked for the Bay, I heard a rumour of a trader who had somehow come across a treasure map. He and his partner scoured the mountains for a year, searching for the cache. Apparently they found gold south of the Medicine Line and were packing it out on horses heading northeast. I suspect the plan was to get it east to Fort Garry and then make their way back to Scotland."

Moses's head snapped up, his eyes flashing. "Scotland! Did this man have red hair?" he demanded.

Milton nodded his head. "Yes, I believe he did, but they never made it to Garry with the gold. Winter was coming and their horses were wearing down carrying the heavy gold. You see, when the Blackfoot realized the bad luck had been dug up, they pursued these men for days before giving up. If there is any truth to this rumour, the traders hid the gold in the Cypress Hills and were able to make it to Fort Garry as winter set in."

"Why did they not come back in the spring?" I wondered aloud.

The captain spoke up. "I might be able to answer that. When I was briefed on this mission, I was told the man that I'm after was fired from the Bay's service because of a killing around late 1832 or early spring of 1833. Seems he got in a drunken fight with his partner and killed him. He was taken by boat north to York Factory and put on a ship for England. The Bay let it be known he was not to come back to Rupert's Land. Sometime after arriving in England, he went to work for the Russians as a spy. The Foreign Office captured him, and he spent the next twenty years in prison. After he was released, he returned to Russia, and there has been no further intelligence on him since."

"I assume his plan was always to somehow get back here and recover that gold. But wouldn't it have been easier for him to have just used a canoe, or even a raft, to sail down the Missouri River to New Orleans when he first dug up the gold in the 1830s?"

"Lots of problems with that," responded Moses. "Two men in a canoe going down the Missouri could easily run into trouble. Hostile Indians would still be a problem at that time. When you get to Saint Louis, some of those wharf rats would notice the low riding canoe and try to steal the gold. Farther down by New Orleans it would be even worse, with river pirates. No sir, two men would have had a hard time hanging onto that gold until they found a ship to England."

Moses continued, "Finding gold is the easiest part. Hanging on to it, now that's much harder. I might have an interest in finding this jasper. If it's who I'm a thinkin' it is, we have some unfinished business." I could see the fire in his eyes.

"Are we sure this is the same man?" I had to ask.

"I'm sure enough," Moses answered back. "I had a friend, Hatcher, who had a map that showed where some gold was buried. His father had stumbled across a cache of gold on a river about a week east and north of Pierre's Hole. This was back in 1806, just a year after the Lewis and Clark expedition. He was with a group of seven men who went west to trap some beaver and make some cash money. They never even got a trap set before they were jumped by some Blackfoot. Hatcher's father was the only survivor and had been on the run for days.

"He managed to stay ahead until the Blackfoot gave up the chase. He was down to one horse, his rifle, a tomahawk, and his Green River. He stopped by a river to rest his horse and cook up what little bacon was left in his saddle bags. Noticing a hollow in the ground, he cleared the grass and dug it out for a fire pit. That's when he hit the gold. Whatever it had been buried in was long gone. But there was a lot more than a tired horse could carry. He put a couple of pounds in his saddlebags. He then refilled the hole, marking a spot with a small cairn of rocks. He rode on, managing to be the only one to make it home to North Carolina. He had always planned on going back to the mountains for the gold but never made it.

"After the elder Hatcher had returned home, he spent the gold wisely and bought into a gunsmithing business. He had started drawing a map, marking the location of the gold to the best of his recollection but was killed before he could finish it. When Hatcher and me went west trapping, he had brought along his father's map. In the end, I reckon this traitorous Scotsman managed to get his hands on that map and figured out where the gold is. I'm pretty sure he's the man responsible for Hatcher's death. When we find him, he's mine!"

Silence descended on the group until Captain Jack addressed Leonard and Milton. "Do either of you two know the Cypress Hills?"

Both nodded their heads. Leonard answered, "We do. There is water and good grass for the stock. We can track this bunch and hopefully get the leader. The hills are a big area, though, and if they disappear in them, they could be hard to find. We could be there in two days with the carts if we pushed hard. There is a lake in the northwest part of the hills where the trees start."

"Who are we most likely to run into for tribes?" the captain queried.

"Depends on where the buffalo are," responded Milton. "If the herd is farther west this year, that's good. If it is more east, we could run into any of the three branches of the Blackfoot or the Sarcee. Even the Kootenai have been known to hunt that far east. Any other tribe we should be able to meet on good terms."

Jack looked to me. "Jim, we need to get on the trail. I know that your wife isn't fully recovered yet. But we can have her travel as comfortably as possible in a cart."

I nodded. "I understand. We signed on to stop these troublemakers."

"Captain," Moses spoke up to get Jack's attention. "I've seen firsthand how crazy gold can make people.

Some get obsessed and will stop at nothing to get it. I propose we declare now that, if we find any, everyone here will get an equal share. That means the Sinclairs, the horse herders, Leonard, your soldiers, my family. Everybody! Our main mission remains to kill this murdering bastard and stop a war."

"Agreed," Jack replied, then turned to Alexander. "Sergeant, prepare the camp to move out. We're going after that turncoat."

I walked over to Celine's tent. Abigail was just opening the flap and saw me approaching. "She's awake and asking for you!"

I think those were the best words I had ever heard. The tight knot in my gut started to ease. My Celine was awake! I flew into the tent and ran to her side. A bandage was still wrapped around her head, with a patch of dried blood showing where the ball had grazed her. Her dark eyes were open, looking up at me, and she had a smile on her face.

"My Lord, girl, you had me worried! I thought I was going to lose you."

Her eyes blinked. She looked a little confused, then asked, "Did we save Judith? I remember a lot of shooting."

I swallowed a lump in my throat, then gently replied, "Yes, Celine, we did rescue Judith. But that was almost two years ago."

"Two years ago? But why are we still on the trail? Didn't you go back home to your farm?"

"We did go home. And you came with us," I answered in a hushed voice. "What do you remember?"

Her eyes closed again for a few seconds, then she opened them and grinned up at me. "Did you ever try to kiss me? I wanted you to."

"Yes, girl, I kissed you. I even married you."

She smiled, but then the puzzled look returned to her face. "We're married? You are my husband? Why don't I remember that?"

Then she winced. "I have such a terrible headache."

"Celine, you've been hurt. But you are going to be okay. I will explain more later. But right now, we have to get travelling. You will be riding in a cart on a pile of blankets. Get some rest now, and don't worry. Moses and your cousin Leonard are part of this outfit."

With a flash of her usual spirit, she retorted, "I will be worrying, Jim. I need you to tell me about the last two years."

"I'll be back as soon as I can. And I will tell you everything. That's a promise."

Celine's eyes then drifted closed, and she fell into a deep sleep. I leaned over and kissed her forehead, then headed out of the tent. Moses had already saddled my horse and was waiting for me.

CHAPTER TWELVE

The expedition was heading south in a little over forty minutes. This time, with a renewed purpose.

If anything, it was drier than ever. Captain Jack had what he called a mercury thermometer. He pulled it out in the middle of the day and recorded the temperature in his journal. A hundred and four degrees, in the shade. Fortunately, Leonard and Milton knew of seeps where the stock could be watered. By late afternoon, we'd approached one such spring. By now, we were well into the sand hills, almost straight south and most of a day from the river forks.

Seein' as Moses, Milton, and myself were scouting ahead, we were the first to arrive at a small spring-fed pool. There was some silver willow taking advantage of the water and growing on the south side. Otherwise, it was surrounded by green grass. The only green in sight for as far as we could see from the heights of our horses. One closer look, however, and all thoughts of a drink vanished.

There in the water were the bloated carcasses of three dead men: one white and two with darker skin. From their bloodstained outfits, it looked like these men had been wounded in one of our earlier encounters.

We silently surveyed the gruesome scene in front of us. Milton was the first to speak. "We can use our picket ropes to haul them out and drag them downwind a couple hundred yards."

"I was thinkin' the same," growled Moses. "We better git 'er done before the carts get here. I'm hoping that at least the oxen can still drink from this."

After sliding down off my horse, I slowly approached the water. I was mid-step when Moses yelled, "STOP! Look down and do not move your leg."

I followed his gaze and could see a thin strip of leather right under where my boot would've touched the ground. Carefully placing my foot down to the rear and backing up, I saw the musket lying on the ground. The barrel was pointed my way, resting on a little mound of dirt. The leather strip was about four inches off the ground, held up by the grass. My eyes traced the length of the strip back to where it wound around a rock, back to the trigger. If my foot had tripped the leather, the musket would have fired.

I took a shaky breath. "That was close. I owe you one."

Moses grinned. "Well, I didn't wanna be the one to be tellin' your missus you done got yer leg shot off!"

After disassembling the trap, we thoroughly searched around the little pond and found two more booby-trapped muskets. Once we were certain that we had found all the traps, Moses carefully unloaded the muskets. Sure enough, they had double charges of powder and a mix of balls and buckshot. The barrels probably would have burst, adding even more shrapnel into the mix. The traitorous Scotsman was doing everything he could to slow us down.

Once we had the putrid bodies hauled away downwind, we could examine the pond. As the water started to clear, the bodies of three dead rattlesnakes became visible. Their venom sacs had been sliced open. We were dealing with the devil incarnate.

We fished the snakes out, hoping the water would clear up enough for future travellers. But that didn't help our current situation. We didn't even want to take the risk of our oxen drinking this.

We mounted up and headed back to meet the approaching carts.

Riding up to the captain, Moses declared, "That sneaky bastard set traps and poisoned the water. We gotta angle a little to the west and bypass that spring. We have enough water for us, but the stock will have to wait."

Captain Jack swore under his breath, then called out, "Sergeant Alexander! We've got to angle the carts off to the southwest. That water hole was booby-trapped and poisoned."

"Aye, Captain," Alexander responded and motioned for the brigade to follow Moses and Milton.

Our carts squealed across the rolling dry prairie for another hour before we stopped to rest the horses and oxen. The stock was picketed to graze. And in the case of the oxen, to chew their cud.

I went to check on Celine and found her awake and resting in the shade of a cart. "Told you I'd be back." I beamed at her. "You're looking better. How are you feeling now?"

"Better. I've been lying here thinking. I am starting to remember a few things," replied Celine. "You were wounded, were you not?"

"I was. But as you can see for yourself, with your nursing, I recovered rather well."

She nodded with a slight smile on her face. Then she became serious. "Why have we stopped where there is no water?"

Sombrely, I told her about the water hole being poisoned but left out the part about the leather trip on the musket.

She struggled to rise. "You need me right now to get us to water!" she stated.

I quickly reassured her. "We'll survive just fine. Moses and Milton have things in hand. You need to rest and get lots of sleep so you can heal. Their plan is to travel through the night when it will be a little cooler. Be rough on the stock, but they should make it."

Celine concentrated with effort. "If we angle off west slightly and are lucky, we might hit a spring. Or maybe a pothole with some water for the animals." Her voice then drifted off; she closed her eyes and fell back to sleep.

Everyone rested as best as they could in the heat. Every cart had people lying under it for shade. Between the heat and worrying about what was ahead of us, I rather doubt anyone got much sleep.

With the sun setting so late at this time of year, it was still light when the cart wheels started rolling. The oxen were none too impressed but had little choice but to plod along. Moses, Milton, Leonard, and myself scouted ahead, spreading out with a half mile between each of us.

Covering a front almost two miles wide, we stood a fair to middlin' chance of finding water, if there was any to be found. This was dry country. The grass was short, but there had to have been some moisture in the spring for it to grow. I wondered if there were ever better years, or if it was always this dry.

Leonard had told me how one of his cousins had been a scout on the Palliser Expedition, a survey party that was concluded only seven years ago. Captain Palliser was a geographer, and Leonard's cousin had seen the map he was making. Palliser's survey party included a geologist, who was also a surgeon. The three remaining men were a botanist, a magnetic observer, and a mathematician who helped navigate with a sextant. The purpose of the expedition was to conduct a scientific survey to determine if there was potential for settlement. I could only assume the people already living here weren't asked what their opinion on the matter was.

According to Leonard's cousin, we were in a large triangle-shaped area that Palliser had marked unfit for settlement, declaring it a dry wasteland. Riding where we were right now, I was inclined to agree. Still, if one had a good spring for water and was careful not to over-graze, cattle ranching might be an option, especially along the rivers. If a person could make a deal with one of the tribes for land in exchange for some beef every year, it might work.

From talking with the Metis, even I realized that the days of hunting buffalo to live were going to end. There were already hungry times because herds of buffalo were getting harder to find. I had even heard stories that Americans were being encouraged to shoot the buffalo out of existence. The herds were nomadic and travelled back and forth across the Medicine Line. So this would have an effect up here in Rupert's Land as well.

I'd been riding in the moonlight for at least an hour by now. The lineback dun I was on was getting restless and wanting to go left. Figuring he had a good reason, I let him have his way. My instincts were proven right. Twenty minutes later, we were at a small spring.

I cautiously scanned the ground before dismounting. Seeing no sign of tracks or traps, I allowed the horse to step to the edge of the water. He lowered his head and thirstily drank his fill. After giving him a few minutes rest, I mounted up. Giving the dun a pat on the neck, I said, "Good job, fella. Now let's go get the others."

Chapter Thirteen

Finding that spring had been a godsend. We may have been able to reach the Cypress Hills without it, but now we were going to make it for sure.

Now that the carts were parked in a circle by the spring and the stock was all grazing, everyone could rest. Captain Jack had two soldiers posted on watch.

I heard Celine stirring in the cart and hurried to look inside. She was awake. She exclaimed excitedly, "Jim, memories are coming back! I remember the farm now. And Grandma. And our wedding day."

"That's my girl! And how is your head feeling?"

"It's not hurting as much as it did before." Then her eyes widened as a thought struck her. "What about Moses's arm? Is it healing? I remember stitching it up after that gang attacked us in the buffalo waller with the chokecherry trees."

"His arm is comin' along just fine," I assured her. "Now, just take it easy, girl. You've got a ways to go yet. Try to get more rest. We'll be starting out for the last leg to the lake later this afternoon."

Celine looked me straight in the eye and demanded, "There is something bothering you, I can tell. What is it?"

Taking my time to answer, I finally replied, "I've been doing a lot of thinking. We're going to have to find a safer line of work. Maybe something that doesn't involve getting shot at. We talked before about getting ourselves our own place. What about cattle ranching out West here somewhere? Maybe we could make a deal with the Cree or the Assiniboine for some land."

She paused thoughtfully before speaking, "That is an idea that just might work. Not right away, but in a few years. I know the buffalo herds are getting smaller. Cattle would do well on this grass if they could survive the winter."

We discussed our future for a few more minutes. Then giving her a hug, I stood up to leave. It was time to go on a scout around the neighbourhood. Like Moses, Captain Jack suspected our Scottish nemesis was already in the Cypress Hills. Not liking surprises though, we wanted to make sure we were alone out here. And there was still the question of the Blackfoot. Where were they? Hopefully, the buffalo were farther west this summer.

I would be searching the area to the southwest, while Moses and Milton would reconnoitre to the southeast. Leonard and one of the soldiers would ride our back trail for a few miles.

I was sliding my Spencer into its scabbard when I heard Sergeant Alexander's rich Scottish brogue. "Could ye be using another rifle with you, lad?"

"Sounds good to me. But hopefully, we won't be needin' to do any shootin'," I replied as I mounted my bay mare. This was her first outing since our initial dust-up with the troublemakers. She was now well-rested and ready to cover some miles.

We were riding through rolling hills with nothing but grass as far as the eye could see. There was hardly any brush, even in the lower spots where water could collect in the spring runoff. Even though we could see the Cypress Hills off to the south, they were still a long, hot, dry ride from where the carts were camped.

Alexander was a man wanting to learn, and he had a lot of questions. "What are yon hills like? They look green from here, so that must mean more water than this barren grassland."

"I've never been in them yet, but my wife has," I responded. "They rise up over the surrounding prairie. She tells me they are about a hundred miles from west to east. Lodgepole pine grow there. Tribes for miles around in every direction cut poles from them for travois and teepees. There are deep coulees and creeks through the hills, with a river flowing out of them to the southeast."

The sergeant nodded. "Sounds like a paradise. Especially compared to where we are right now."

I laughed. "There is one drawback, though. There's a whole passel of grizzly bears think it's paradise too."

No sooner had I finished speaking than a shot rang out somewhere ahead of us. Cautiously, we rode up a knoll, dismounting before the crest. I handed my reins to Alexander, then crawled up to peer over the rise.

Two men, their horses obviously played out, were being chased by a group of riders. The man in front turned back in his saddle and took a shot at the attackers. They were quickly losing ground to their pursuers; barely fifty yards separated the two groups now. The two fellers in the lead were about a hundred and fifty yards away, heading right towards me. They were close enough now that I could see that the jaspers doing the chasing were all too familiar.

Alexander crawled up beside me, saying, "I hobbled the horses." Being no fool, he also instantly recognized the renegades after the two men. I raised my Spencer and started firing. My second shot dropped a horse and sent its rider flying through the air. Don't think the flying hurt him, but the landing looked mighty rough.

Alexander, being a seasoned soldier, followed the first rule of an infantryman when attacked by cavalry. Sighting down the long barrel of the Snyder Enfield, he shot another horse. The rider was crushed under the horse when it somersaulted. He was done for.

By now, we had the attention of both groups. Alexander and I continued firing at the renegades. I shot one and saw him flinch hard then roll off his horse, almost in slow motion. The sergeant also hit one, but he managed to stay in his saddle. That seemed to be the final straw. Scooping up the wounded feller, the remaining six renegades fled off to the southwest.

The men who had been chased rode up to us. Looked to me that we had saved two old mountain men.

The first one climbed off his lathered-up horse. He was tall and slim, with a short stubble of a beard. Grey hair showed out the bottom of a seven-inch stovepipe hat. He was wearing brown striped pants and run-down boots, with a buckskin shirt that appeared to be about as old and worn out as he was, finishing off his apparel. Looked to me he was packin' a mountain rifle, single-shot pistol, Green River, and a 'hawk. Just like Moses had carried before we got the newer hardware.

"We sure owe you fellas a heap of thanks! Our horses were just about done for," he exclaimed, pumping our hands.

The second rider groaned and then started to slide off his horse. Alexander managed to catch him and ease him to the ground. A dark stain was forming on the lower leg of his buckskin leggings.

"He's losing blood!" snapped Alexander. He pulled a rag out of his pocket and quickly wrapped it above the wound, pulling it as tight as he could. "Lad, could you bring my saddlebags? I've got bandages in there."

I ran downhill to the horses. After untying the saddlebags, I scurried back up the hill to help the sergeant tend to the wound.

One thing about the old soldier, he knew what he was doing. He had me take the ramrod from his rifle, and he put it under the cloth wrapped around the wound. Then, twisting the ramrod to tighten the cloth, he made a tourniquet. Soon, the bleeding had stopped.

I spoke up. "We'll have to get him back to the carts. The Sinclair wives will give him as good a chance as he's gonna get. I'll hold him on my horse in front of me. You two lift him up."

The tall old trapper protested. "I can carry him with me."

I shook my head. "Your horse ain't gonna carry double very far. Mine's in better shape. Let's just get your friend to our carts. By the way, I'm Jim Munro. And that's Sergeant Alexander of the British Army."

"They call me Deacon," he replied. Then, motioning to his friend, "That's Joseph Ford, but all we ever called him was Oneida. He's a good man and a loyal friend. There were three of us when we first set out. But Dexter Perkins was killed when those bastards first jumped us earlier today."

We all mounted and started making our way back to camp. Deacon rode up beside me. "I knew a James Munro many years ago. We all called him Moses on account of his white hair. Any chance you kin of his?"

I gave a little chuckle. "He's my grandfather. You'll be seein' him soon enough. He's scouting to the east but should be back at the camp soon."

Deacon slapped his leg. "Well, I'll be jiggered! Don't that beat all? Moses's grandson saved our hides.

"What are you fellers doing up in Rupert's Land? Last I heard, Moses was guiding wagon trains to the Oregon country."

I replied, "It's a long story. Right now, we hold constable commissions from Governor MacTavish himself. We're after some troublemakers who have been raising cane up here, trying to start a war. We're scouting for some soldiers sent from England to hunt them down. Turns out they are the same renegades who you just tangled with."

I paused and eyed the old codger. "So what brings you up here?"

"Well, we 'acquired' some horses down in the Montana Territory. Figured to trade them to the Hudson Bay at Fort Qu'Appelle. But them bastards stole our horses and then set to kill us."

I thought to myself, how did they 'acquire' horses? And why would they bring them all the way to Qu'Appelle to trade? Fort Benton in Montana was much closer. Something in the old man's story wasn't adding up. But I had no further time to ponder on it. The wounded man had collapsed into unconsciousness and was dead weight to keep in front of me on the saddle. We needed to get him back to camp before it was too late.

CHAPTER FOURTEEN

As soon as we reached camp, I rushed the Oneida over to the Sinclair ladies. They immediately had the wounded man moved into a cart, where they commenced treating him.

The carts were already hitched to the oxen, ready to make the last dry stretch. Then we'd be in the green Cypress Hills with its lake full of cool water. Celine was already mounted on her horse, ready to travel.

"What in tarnation are you doing, girl? You need to be resting!" I exclaimed.

"Jim Munro, I only have a little bit of a headache now. I'm not wounded or bleeding. I am going to ride this horse, and you are going to be good with it!"

Moses's voice chimed in from behind me. "Losing arguments with that girl is gettin' to be habit formin', if you ask me." He laughed. I hadn't seen him ride into camp.

I looked at Celine's determined face. "At least stay close to me so I can keep an eye on you."

"I'll be right beside you. You can count on it," she promised, with that mischievous grin she so often gave me.

We then heard a loud holler from Moses, which reverberated across the whole cart brigade. "Since when did we start travelling with horse thieves?" he thundered.

"Now Munro, don't be gettin' yer dander in an uproar. Yer grandson saved Oneida's and my hides today. Oneida's wounded and needed medical attention." Deacon carried on, "And besides, it was our horses that got stole!"

"Ya, and who'd you steal the horses offen?" snapped Moses.

"I'll have you know we acquired them from the Gros Ventre."

"Did anybody happen to write you a bill of sale when you was acquiring these horses?" Moses sarcastically enquired.

"Them Gros Ventre couldn't read and write."

I think about then the only thing keeping Moses from cussing a blue streak was the presence of ladies.

"Oh, for God's sake! As if we don't have enough problems, now we're gonna have a bunch of Indians show up on the warpath 'cuz you couldn't resist stealing their horses," roared Moses.

By now, everyone in the camp was watching the carryings on with interest. Captain Jack was being briefed by Alexander when the ruckus started.

Jack strode over. "I take it you two are acquaintances."

"We trapped in the mountains back in the day," grumbled Moses. "Deacon here is the only man I ever knew that could steal horses from the Crow."

"How do you do, Captain?" Deacon broke in. "No need to worry, them Gros Ventres won't be coming after us anyway. They'll be after the jaspers who stole them horses from us."

He then turned to Moses, tears forming at the corners of his eyes. "Moses, they done killed Dexter when they attacked us."

Moses went quiet. And then sombrely spoke. "Jed Smith, Fitzpatrick, Hatcher, Smiley, Milt Sublette, Hugh Glass and now Dexter. Gettin' to be fewer of us all the time."

He addressed Captain Jack. "Once we get these carts headed for that lake, I'll take Deacon and we'll go bury Dexter proper."

Moses glowered at Deacon. "I hate to admit it, but I'd probably have saved your thievin' hide too. You'd better be right about them Gros Ventres not chasing you for their horses. Not much we can do about that right now anyway."

He then turned to Captain Jack and said, "We better start rolling. It's gonna be a long dry haul till we get to that water."

Chapter Fifteen

A cloud of dust hung over us as the carts rolled southward. I was at the lead of the carts. Celine was holding up well and stayed close to me. By now, all the soldiers had adopted Celine as their little sister. Later, when I had to be out scouting, I knew I could trust that one of them would be keeping an eye on her, making sure she was safe.

Alexander rode up front with us. Moses and Deacon had ridden out a quarter mile ahead, watching for any sign of an ambush. The Sinclair wives rode beside the cart with the Oneida in it. Travelling was going to be rough on him, but we had no choice but to keep moving. We needed to catch up to this band of Asians and their traitorous leader and put a stop to their plans. And, I had to be honest, a little bit of that gold would come in mighty handy for our family as well.

Moses dropped back, saying as he rode up, "I'm gonna grab a shovel off the tool cart. Deacon and me will veer off right and go bury Dexter."

"Need help?" Alexander and I both asked.

"No, we'll do it," Moses solemnly said. "He was our friend."

I waved to Moses. "I'll scout ahead while you do that."

Once they had ridden off, Alexander offered, "You should have someone with you. I'll ride along." Catching my glance towards Celine, he proposed, "I'll have Adams and O'Riley keep an eye on her." Then added, "If that's alright with you, ma'am?"

"For today. But in a couple of days, I will be riding with my husband, even if he's scouting!" Then, giving me a wink and a saucy smile, she dropped back to travel beside the carts.

Once we were ahead of the carts and well out of earshot, the sergeant started speaking. "The captain asked me to have a word with you. He's wondering if you trust that man, Deacon?"

I grinned back at him. "In the words of my grandfather, not as far as I can throw him. That's why he took Deacon with him today. Moses claimed Deacon was like a man who lived for the drink, only Deacon's drink was good horses. Didn't seem to steal anything else. But Moses always kept an eye on his horse whenever he was around." I paused before adding, "We ain't gonna mention the gold to him either."

Even after the sun went down past the horizon, it barely cooled down. We had enough light from the moon to work our way south through the hills. The squeals of the carts carried even farther in the still night air. I'm sure our enemies had to know exactly where we were. No one ever snuck around in a Red River cart.

It was a rough, dirty, tired-looking crew that rolled up to the shores of the lake early the next afternoon. People's clothes were stained from head to toe with dust and sweat, brown streaks dripping from their faces and necks. The horses and oxen were all lathered, their heads hanging down in exhaustion.

We had made it! It was hard to believe that this place could exist in the middle of the barren prairie. The grass was green and lush around the lake. Most of the hills were covered in trees. And the water was crystal clear. Even with the grizzly bears, this was a paradise.

After tending to the stock, we all ran into the lake. It was cool and refreshing after the unending heat of the past few days. It felt so good to get the trail dust off! People were laughing and smiling and even playfully splashing water at each other as they washed.

It was a short reprieve, though. After everyone had cleaned up, we had a job to do. The wounded Oneida had passed away about an hour before our arrival. He had lost too much blood to survive, in spite of the care of the Sinclair ladies.

We buried him under some pine trees on a slope overlooking the lake. We helped Deacon gather some rocks, and after we made a cairn over the grave, Captain Jack read some words from the Good Book. Another of the old mountain men had gone under.

Moses, Leonard, and one of the soldiers took first watch. The rest of us lay our blankets under the carts and slept. Celine snuggled up close to me when I joined her. I don't think either of us moved for two hours. The last few days had been rough, but we had made it. She was feeling better but was not her full energetic self yet. Here, by the lake, she would recover.

The next morning, we moved the carts around to the south side of the lake. Finding a level spot, we set about building a camp. The carts were placed in a defensible circle, with the tents pitched within. There was room to protect the stock as well if trouble showed up.

So far, we had been lucky. There hadn't been any sign of Blackfoot yet. They could well be hunting farther west this year. However, when it came to the Gros Ventre, we were under no illusions. They would be after their horses. And if they couldn't find theirs, our horses would fill their needs. We needed to make sure we had enough men in the camp for defence at all times.

After breakfast, Moses glanced sideways at Celine and me, then nodded. He got up and stretched, saying, "Gotta go check on my Appaloosa."

We stood up as well. "We'll come with you." Then all three of us made our way over to the horses.

Moses was clearly agitated. "If something happens to me, don't turn your back on Deacon. Hatcher never trusted him, even when we left Saint Louis the first time with Ashley's Hundred.

"Last night, I remembered something. Not too long before he died, Hatcher told me that Deacon was a cousin of his. The two sides of the family didn't get along at all. Hatcher always figured Deacon's family had something to do with his father's death." He paused. "How that matters now is that Deacon probably knows about the map. He ain't stupid. He'll have figured out who we're after."

"That means he knows there might be some gold out here as well," thoughtfully commented Celine.

"Yep." Moses continued, "And he'll be figuring on getting it for himself."

"What should we be doing about him for now?" I wondered aloud.

"We just keep our eyes peeled on him. I'd like to let the Gros Ventre have him if they show up, but I guess we can't do that," muttered Moses before growling, "no matter how appealing the idea."

Celine spoke up. "Can we trust the soldiers?"

"I would be inclined to," I answered slowly. "But we'd better keep our eyes and ears open. The Sinclairs and Leonard we can trust. I think Milton as well."

Moses started walking. "Best be headin' back to camp. Don't want Deacon thinkin' we're on to him."

After a war council with Captain Jack and Alexander, we decided to have two groups—Captain Jack called them squads—out looking for sign. The first group would consist of Moses, Deacon, Captain Jack, and Becker Wright. Leonard, Sergeant Alexander, and John Sinclair would be with me. All of us would ride around the north side of the lake.

The troublemakers, travelling with their newly acquired horses, would leave a lot of tracks. We had decided that if there were no tracks, we would split up. My squad would head west, and Moses's would head east. It seemed simple enough, but sometimes simple can get mighty complicated.

An hour after leaving camp, it was Leonard who found hoofprints on the west side of the lake where the renegades had watered their horses. They had been there a day ahead of us. The tracks led up the slope, gradually curving east and then heading southeast. The killers and horses had only been five hundred yards south of where our encampment was now!

By midday, we had come out onto the plateau. Here was a grassland with scattered trees, although the grass differed from the dry semi-arid rolling prairie we had travelled across on our way to these hills. There seemed to be more variety, and of course, it was green. Every time we stopped for a break, the horses grabbed a bite. Same as with every little stream we came to, they had to have a drink. Just as it was a paradise for us two-legged folk, the four-legged kind found it just as appealing.

We stopped to rest the horses by one of the bluffs at the head of a coulee. Moses motioned me aside. "Now might be a good time to split up. Notice how there's not as many tracks? Looks to me like two or three slipped away from the bunch. It would have been easy enough to do as they rode by the trees at the head of the last coulee we rode past. Could be that Scotsman sneaking off for the gold. Or a couple breaking off to lead us on a wild goose chase."

"Could be either," I agreed. "If he started scattering his men, it would make it mighty tough to follow. If he finds the gold, we don't know how he plans on returning home with it. Leonard tells me the headwaters of a small river are a long day and a half southeast of here. That river flows into the Milk. He'd end up in the Mississippi. It would still be risky, but two or three reliable men would have a chance. Not near as many hostile tribes as thirty years ago. The Lakota are farther west, attacking army forts and gold miners."

"Might be how he plans on getting out. Depends on where the gold is," said Moses. "Thirty years ago, it sounds like he was planning on wintering at Fort Garry and returning for the gold in the spring. I think that means the gold is on the north or northeast side of these hills."

I thought for a minute. "Do you want to follow the riders that slipped away at the coulee then? I'll keep following the main bunch and hopefully find out if that Scotsman is still with them."

Moses nodded. "Sounds as good a plan as any. Let's run it by Captain Jack. But Jim, don't tangle with that bunch. If he's still with them, just follow. I'll know within a day if I'm on the right trail. If I'm not back with you in two days, come find me."

CHAPTER SIXTEEN

After splitting up, my outfit continued following the tracks. Late in the afternoon, Leonard held up his hand. Once we stopped moving, the faint sounds of distant gunfire could be heard.

"It's ahead of us. Maybe four miles, maybe a little more," stated Leonard.

"Hope our killers didn't find someone else to raid," I commented. "We better check it out. Someone may need our help."

We headed towards the sound of the gunfire for fifteen minutes, and then it stopped.

Alexander rode up beside me. "Hopefully, someone drove that pack of thieves and killers off."

I nodded back to him. "We can hope. It sure sounded like one hell of a fight."

Soon we were approaching the end of another coulee.

Leaving our horses with the sergeant and Sinclair, Leonard and myself crawled to the crest of the hill and peered over. Below us, on a level area of open ground, was the grisly sight of a battlefield. It was deathly quiet. We counted nine bodies. Taking my time, I used Pa's field glasses to give the area around the bodies a thorough scan. From what I could tell, these were the bodies of the Asians we had been trailing. And all of them were scalped.

I spotted one more body lying a little east of the rest. He, too, had been scalped. Looked like he had tried to make a break for it, but his luck had run out.

I commented to Leonard, "If I was guessing, I would say the Gros Ventre just got their horses back. And a few more to boot!"

Moses had taught me to always be patient and cautious. So I lifted Pa's glasses to my eyes and studied the carnage below one more time.

I whispered to Leonard, "Look at the tree line across from us. Can you see a feller peekin' out from behind a tree?"

I handed him Pa's glasses. Putting them to his eyes, he looked to where I had pointed. "I can. And he has a gun!" Leonard continued watching and then murmured, "He just moved a bit, and I can see he's got an arrow stuck in his shoulder!"

"Looks like he's all that's left of our troublemakers," I whispered. "It sure would be nice to catch that jasper over yonder alive."

Leonard and I then crawled back from the ridgeline and made our way back to our companions, where I proceeded to update Alexander and Sinclair.

"Well, fellas, things just got interesting. Most of our renegades are now scalped carcasses laying out in the meadow below us. Only one is still alive, and he's got an arrow in him. He's hunkered down in the treeline just opposite from us. If we stay below the skyline, we can work our way around behind him. We just have to ride back around where the coulee starts to drop off. Once on the far side, we'll crawl over the crest. If he's still there, we'll have him. Don't shoot him if at all possible."

There are those rare occasions when a plan is made, and it actually works. We had spread apart a few yards before we all crawled over the ridge. Our quarry, if he could be called that, was still behind his tree. He was thirty yards directly in front of Alexander.

"Don't move," I yelled at him. "We're lawmen, and we got four rifles covering you."

His head jerked around, and he could see we weren't foolin'. He let the trade musket he was holding slip to the ground, begging, "Just don't let those savages have me."

"From what I've seen, laddie, you're in no position to be callin' anyone a savage," snapped the old sergeant. "Way I see things, those Indians were just getting their horses back. Your bunch attacked three old men with a small herd of horses. Only problem for you, the horses had been stolen earlier from the Gros Ventres."

Looking closely at the wounded man, I recognized him. He was the blond-haired leader of that bunch we'd had our first shooting scrape with. "That arrow didn't put the only hole in your sorry carcass, did it?" I grilled him.

"No, I got shot a few days back by some bushwhackers."

"Your memory must not be serving you well. Have a real good gander at me."

The man's eyes widened as he realized who I was. "You! You shot me."

"I did. Only *you* were trying to kill us. Didn't work out too well for you, did it? Cost you some men. Then your boss man tried to kill us again after that, and my wife got grazed on the side of the head. If she ain't feelin' better when we get back to camp, I'll be in a foul mood. Looks like you're the only one left I can take revenge on.

"By the looks of the tracks, your leader and a couple of his favourites slipped off on their own. I'd bet my constable's wages he didn't tell the rest of you, did he? But don't feel too bad for yourself," I consoled him. "I'm pretty sure the fellers riding with him won't see home again. From what I can tell, people partnered up with him have a bad habit of dying."

The man's head hung dejectedly. "But what about me? You said you was law. You can't kill me. You have to help me! At least get this arrow out of me!" wailed the desperado.

Kneeling down, I cut away the filthy bandage that was covering the bullet hole I'd put in him. It was oozing pus and starting to show green around the wound. The sickly smell of death was already upon this sorry creature. Another painful day, at the most, was all he had left.

"Tell me everything you know about this operation, and I'll do what I can for you."

He started talking feverishly. "Me and five other fellers hired on with Graham when he came through the mountains. We was at a mining camp and flat busted. Said he had three, twenty-five-pound bags of gold nuggets buried in the Cypress Hills. He told us he was hired to cause a big ruckus on the prairie to get some injuns fightin'. Said he'd pay extra for helping with that. You gotta understand—we were broke, and it seemed like easy money. And he said he was going to pay us in gold!"

"Oh, I understand completely," I replied in a dangerously calm voice. "You needed money and were too lazy to look for work. So you figgered that gave you the right to go around shooting innocent people to start a war. I've got more news for you, pardner. This Graham never intended on paying you a dime."

He whimpered, "I done told you everythin' I know. You still gonna help me?"

"I told you I'd do what I could for you." I sombrely nodded to Alexander, and he drew his pistol.

CHAPTER SEVENTEEN

We watered the horses in the meadow where the Gros Ventres had recovered their horses. We took a few minutes to check over the bodies. All had been scalped, with anything of use having been already picked up. Sometimes being a hired gun just don't work out.

Being as it was later in June, we had enough daylight left to get in a few more hours of travelling. It wouldn't get us caught up to Moses's crew, but it would help.

After we were out of the meadow of death, Alexander, who was riding beside me, asked, "How is it the Gros Ventres never attacked us?"

It was Leonard who answered. "I think there were two reasons. They might have had a scout close enough to see you shooting with your carbine when you saved Deacon's sorry hide. Plus, we hadn't stolen their horses. They figured out the trail those thieving killers were taking. And set up a well-executed ambush."

"They could still follow around and get us, couldn't they?" questioned the sergeant.

"They could, but I don't think they will," I answered. "On the plains, it's buffalo hunting time. They have their own horses back, plus a few extra. And I don't think they lost anybody. They're ahead of the game, and they have people to feed. I remember Moses telling me that the Gros Ventres were thinned out with smallpox. They need their warriors, and this area is still claimed by the Blackfoot. I reckon they figured to git while the gittin' was good."

We followed our backtrail until the sun started to fall behind the horizon. It didn't take long until we had the kettle boiling. Once we had washed down some pemmican with tea, it was time to turn in. I took the middle watch, figuring if anything was going to happen, that's when it would. Fortunately, the night passed with no interruptions.

Morning came, and once we washed down more pemmican with boiling tea, we mounted up. Only an hour after setting out, we reached the head of the coulee, where Moses's squad had split off, following the tracks that had slipped away from the main crowd of renegades.

For roughly three miles, we followed a narrow trail downhill, with steep tree-lined walls. Gradually, the floor of this coulee widened out enough you could call it a small valley. The whole time we had been travelling east, following a small stream of water. It gradually increased in size as it was joined by little tributaries, coming down from every ravine that branched out from the valley.

That was what amazed me so much about these hills. The amount of water! After the dry prairie where water was scarce, this was heaven.

I figured we had travelled roughly four hours by the time we made our way to the valley floor. Here, there were large patches of tall grass on both sides of the trail. It was the buzzing of flies that gave us our first clue. Then, the smell of death. Rounding a slight curve in the trail, we came across a dead horse. Its head had been almost ripped off. Beside the dead horse lay the tangled and torn remains of a man.

Surveying the scene in front of him, Alexander sadly affirmed, "That's Private Wright." It looked like Moses's crew had run into some serious trouble.

"A grizzly bear?" he asked me.

I nodded to the sergeant. "Yeah. A big one."

I swallowed a lump in my throat. Where on earth was Moses?

Everyone had their rifles out. Suddenly there was a movement off in the trees! The tension in the air was so thick you could have cut it with a knife.

"Wait, don't shoot! It's me, Jack."

The captain limped out of the trees, leaning on his rifle as a crutch. He was deathly pale and swayed as he fought to stay upright. His left leg was a raw and bloody mess. His clothes were shredded and in tatters.

"Could you lads help me? I seem to have gotten myself scratched." Then he collapsed in a heap to the ground.

Leaving the other three men to look after Jack, I carefully scouted around the surrounding area, looking for Moses.

Moving slowly, I heard the buzzing of flies ahead in the tall grass. My heart started racing faster than the first time I was shot at. God, don't let it be Moses!

I made my way through the brush with my carbine at the ready. The carcass of the grizzly came into view. He was quite dead. Looking around where the foliage was trampled, I could see a boot. Moses's boot! Slowly, I parted the tall grass and looked down at him. He was lying motionless, face down. Was he dead? Oh Lord, not now.

Kneeling beside him, I gently rolled him over. I could see no signs of blood.

Then Moses groaned, and his eyes fluttered open. "Jim, you found us! My Lord, my head aches."

A rush of relief came over me. He was alive! "Whoa, just take it easy. The bear must have got a good hit on you before he died."

"Bear, no. I plugged him. Took all seven bullets in my carbine plus one from Deacon's rifle."

Moses sat up slowly to look around. "He's not here, is he? Bastard must've hit me from behind with his rifle butt."

"No sign of Deacon. He's gone. Looks like he took your carbine and pistol as well," I answered. "I'm thinkin' we better get you and Jack back to camp. Sinclair is doing what he can for him, but the quicker the ladies and Celine can work on him, the better. And you are in no shape to chase after anybody right now, even if we can find your horse."

For a second, I thought Moses was going to argue. But he eventually nodded his head, wincing as he did so. We got lucky and found Moses's Appaloosa a couple hundred yards away. Captain Jack's horse was gone, either grabbed by Deacon or run off somewhere.

Leonard and Sinclair had been busy making a travois for the captain. They cut down and stripped the branches off two lodgepole pines. Then they used the blankets from a couple of our bedrolls. While they were finishing, I helped Alexander bury what was left of Becker Wright.

Leonard came over to me. "Jim, Moses's app is the freshest horse. He's had the saddle on for all night, but it can be hauled on the travois. I could ride bareback and make it back to camp in as little as four hours. I can bring a couple of fresh horses and meet you on the trail. With any luck, we'll have everyone back to the camp by nightfall."

I nodded. "Sounds good to me."

Leonard headed out, and the rest of us started the slow journey back to camp. Being a horse short, Alexander, Sinclair, and myself took turns walking. Fortunately, it wasn't as hot in the hills as on the surrounding prairie. Trees and elevation made all the difference.

We had to stop often, as Moses needed to rest. Jack was in a lot of pain but mercifully passed out and was unconscious for most of the trip. Progress was slow, but we kept going. Every step got us closer to camp.

It was late afternoon when we met up with Leonard, who was returning with some fresh horses. And Celine!

Lord, it was good to see her! She dismounted and raced over to me, pulling me into a deep hug. "Thank heavens, you are okay! I was worried the whole time you were gone!"

She then spotted Moses, who was resting on the ground. She exclaimed anxiously, "What happened? How badly is he hurt?"

"He took a hit on the ol' noggin, but he should be feeling better in a few days. It's Captain Jack who needs your attention the most. He got mauled by a grizzly. Thank heavens you're here. We didn't know that you were coming with Leonard."

"I was needed. Now I must get to work." She immediately began pulling bandages and supplies out of her saddlebag and bent over the captain.

What a woman! I was proud of her. She must still have a hell of a headache but rode out here in spite of how she felt. Whenever the going got tough, she was there.

After washing his wounds with alcohol, she then commenced to stitch him back together. I'll say this for him—Jack was as tough as they come. He came to while she was doctoring, and there was barely a whimper from him.

Leonard and Sinclair had been busy fashioning another travois for Moses. By the time Celine had Jack sewn and bandaged, we were ready to continue our journey.

We travelled slowly. It was a long, arduous process, as we were trying not to jostle the two injured men on the travois any more than necessary. The sun was already setting by the time our exhausted group made our way into camp. The Sinclair ladies rushed to take over the care of Moses and Captain Jack. The rest of us wearily collapsed into our bedrolls and into a dreamless sleep. Deacon and Graham would just have to wait until tomorrow.

Chapter Eighteen

The sun was rising when I crawled out of our tent. Other than the men on watch, the only people already up were the Sinclair ladies and Celine. Moses was still in a deep sleep but breathing well. He had been lucky. If Deacon had hit him harder, he might well have been dead.

I got to thinking on how this Graham would get his gold to civilization. If he was content with living rich in America, all he had to do was get to the Missouri River. The Whitemud River flows out southeast from these hills into the Milk, which flows into the Missouri. He could then canoe to Omaha or Kansas City. If he was lucky, he could maybe catch a steamboat somewhere along the river. But…heavy sacks of gold would draw attention. Once he got to a bank, he was in the clear. It was getting heavy sacks of gold to a bank without getting robbed or killed that was the tricky part.

There would be less chance of being robbed if he followed rivers in Rupert's Land. Could it be done, though? I would have to ask Celine.

After a breakfast of elk steak (Milton had bagged a yearling elk while we were away), I cleaned my carbine. Then I asked Celine if she'd like to ride up to a high lookout point to see what, if anything, was happening out on the prairie. She was more than happy to accompany me, especially after the last few days.

I had come close to losing her. An inch farther to the right, and that musket ball would have killed her. Now she was on a horse beside me, and life was good.

"Jim," she asked, "what do we do now? The man who's been causing all the trouble got away again. Can we even catch him? We don't need the gold as long as we have each other."

"You're right, my girl, we don't need gold. I need to talk to Moses when he comes around. He wants this Graham bad. And we both want Deacon. I should never have saved his hide, but it's too late now."

We rode out onto a point of land that overlooked the prairie for miles. Pulling Pa's field glasses from my saddlebag, I scanned the horizon from the northeast around to the west.

"Oh no!" I gasped. I handed the glasses to Celine. "Look west. What do you see?"

She surveyed the landscape for a minute before commenting, "Buffalo, pretty big herd, a few hundred at least. Looks like they are slowly grazing their way towards us." She continued staring through the lenses. "It's hard to tell for sure, but off to the south of the buffalo, it looks like a hunting party."

"I'll take your word for it. We've got to get back and strike the camp. If that's Blackfoot, they ain't gonna like us here. Could get the idea we're here to hunt buffalo."

"Oui," she agreed. "We've got to warn the others."

Everyone stared as, forty-five minutes later, we galloped into the encampment.

Riding up to Alexander, we dismounted. "We may be having company in a day or two. I'm a thinkin' it's company that we don't want."

He immediately understood what I meant. "Blackfoot, I presume?"

"Very possibly. We got a pretty big herd of buffalo making their way towards us from the west. Through the field glasses, Celine thought she spotted mounted Indians behind the buffalo. They're probably hoping to hunt them buffalo once they get closer to the hills. Lots of water and plenty of wood for drying racks and fires here."

Alexander thought for a minute before answering me. "I guess I'm officially in charge now, seeing as the captain hasn't awoken yet." He turned and barked a loud command. "Could I have everyone over here, except young Gerald? He can stay guarding the stock."

Looking over our assembled group, I counted twelve shooters. That included Celine and Moses, if he woke up in any shape to be in a scrap.

The sergeant addressed everyone. "We have possible hostiles approaching behind a herd of buffalo. I think it's time we pulled out for Garry. Any ideas on a quicker route?"

Mark Sinclair spoke up. "We could go east on the north side of the hills. Keeps us moving away from the buffalo and the Blackfoot following them. Then, we meet up with the cart trail to Fort Qu'Appelle. It'll be dry out on the prairie, but the trail follows its course for a reason. Water is usually available."

Turning to Leonard, I inquired, "Seein' as we've got pretty much everything unloaded, how soon do you think we could be ready to roll?"

"Give us two hours, and there won't be much left to pack up." He paused, considering. "Are we going to need to make room on carts for the two injured men?" he asked.

"You won't be needin' no room on a cart for me!"

I spun around to see Moses had walked up behind me. I wouldn't say he looked his best, but that was Scots-Irish fighting blood flowing through his veins. His ancestors had fought from southwestern Scotland to Ulster, then Pennsylvania, down through the Shenandoah Valley and on into the Carolinas. His family had fought in every war, from Queen Anne's War to the Revolution. His grandfather and father had travelled a hundred miles to fight at Kings Mountain in 1780. He'd gone west to trap beaver with Ashley's Hundred in 1822. Moses had lived in the mountains, fought with and against Indians, and had a Shoshone wife murdered. He'd hunted down her killers and carried on with life. It'd take more than a knock on the head to keep him down.

I shook my head in disbelief. "How's that thick skull feeling?

"I've been hurt worse," he growled. Then he grinned. "I'm feelin' a whole heap better since those Sinclair ladies poured half a gallon of willow bark tea down my throat. I can ride just fine. And shoot too, if need be."

I thought to myself, I bet that explains Celine's 'recovery' too.

Moses was carrying his old Nazareth mountain rifle and the spare Colt revolver. We'd packed a few spare guns when we started out from Fort Garry. My Warner carbine was with us as well as our smoothbore musket. The musket had been cut down to eighteen inches. Loaded with a mix of .36 calibre pistol balls and double ought buckshot, that old gun could cut quite a swath.

In ten minutes under two hours, we had all the carts ready to roll. Leonard's people had hitched the carts to the oxen while Celine, myself, and Alexander's soldiers struck the tents and loaded them.

Leonard and Milton scouted a half mile ahead of the brigade. The soldiers rode along both sides of the carts, alert for trouble. Moses, Celine, and I followed a half mile behind to cover our backtrail.

Once we had dropped back far enough from the carts, I had to ask, "Moses, how did you get jumped by the grizz?"

"I couldn't smell him until it was too late. We had the lightest of a breeze at our backs. When we rounded a slight bend in the tall grass, we startled him eating his dinner. He was feeding on a man's carcass.

"Everything happened so fast after that. By the time I had my carbine up to shoot, the grizz had already ripped into Private Wright and his horse. Captain Jack went down fighting. He put a couple pistol balls in the bear before he was attacked. I heard Deacon's mountain rifle fire off to my left. I emptied my carbine, levering bullets into that bear as fast as I could. Then the next thing I remember is you kneeling over me."

I remarked, "I never seen another body. I quit looking when I found you. I'm thinkin' it was one of Graham's companions. I'd bet good money he has plans for his other companion after he finds the gold too."

"God, it would've been nice to put a bullet in that Scotsman," muttered Moses. "Now it's lookin' like he got away again. For over thirty years, I've wanted to kill that bastard for what I had to do."

"What did you have to do?" Celine quietly whispered.

Moses looked off towards the mountains, before slowly answering. "We'd wintered with the Shoshone. Deacon, the Oneida, Dexter Perkins, Smiley Bennett, Hatcher, and me. Spring came early that year. I usually trapped with Hatcher, but Dexter and Smiley had got in a fight over a woman. Hatch and me decided we'd split them up. I'd follow a stream with Dexter, and Hatch would take Smiley farther north and east. I knew about the map, but I didn't have much faith in it. Hatch never gave up, though, and that's why he was farther east than we usually went.

"Then the storm hit. Dexter and myself had built a crude shelter that we hurriedly covered with spruce boughs. We barely managed to survive for the two days of the storm. If our horses hadn't been in the shelter with us, I think we'd have frozen to death.

"Once the storm passed, Dexter rode the stream, checking our traps. It took me two days to get to where Hatch and Smiley had made their camp. I found what was left of Smiley by a stream, not far from their base. I could tell by the tracks it was a raiding party, most likely Blackfoot. They had Hatch, so I followed to see if I could rescue him. When I caught up, it was too late."

"Hatcher was dead," I murmured.

"No, worse." Moses stopped speaking for a moment, haunted by the memory. He wiped at his eyes, then continued. "Hatch was still alive and being tortured! At least what was left of him. I was hidden under a spruce tree, three hundred yards away from him. He was screaming in agony. His torturer was getting ready to burn his eyes out when Hatch screamed, 'DO IT, MUNRO!' How he knew I was there, I'll never know. Maybe he was just hoping. I couldn't let his agony continue. And so… I shot my best friend. After I fired, the torturer turned his head. And I could see he had the red beard of a white man!

"There was nothing more I could do but get on my horse and get the hell out of that valley. Fortunately, nobody followed."

Celine and I both had tears in our eyes.

"You did what you had to do," Celine consoled him.

"You'd have been dead, too, if you stuck around," I stated.

More tears fell from Moses's eyes. "Don't make it any easier, Jim."

"It was when Milton told the story about the gold that I realized why Smiley and Hatch had been tortured. Graham wanted to know where to start looking for the gold. But they didn't know where it was. The map showed the streams, but not all the mountains around where the gold was." Moses paused. "Hatch's dad was killed before he marked down which valley the stream was in."

Something had been nagging in the back of my mind for days. "But Deacon did?"

"Deacon was diggin' in Hatcher's pack one night. When I caught him, he just let on he'd mistaken it for his. This was a year before Hatch and Smiley went under. I forgot about that until all this talk about the gold came up. If'n I was a gambling man, I'd bet Deacon seen the map and kept quiet until meeting up with this Graham at rendezvous. Maybe Deacon already knew him, or maybe they just met and recognized each other's black heart.

"I already owe Deacon for my headache. And he's gonna pay for his part in all this treachery. Once the carts are safely out of reach of the Blackfoot, I'm going hunting for him."

"Well, you won't be going alone because I'm going with you," I declared.

"I can't drag you into this. This is an old piece of unfinished business on my part. You don't need to be caught up in this."

"Well," I remarked, "Looks to me like we already are. You ain't in any shape to be traipsing around lookin' for a fight all by your own self! I'll be goin' with you, and there won't be any negotiatin' on the matter!"

"That's good there's no more negotiating!" spoke up Celine, her dark eyes glowing with fire, "because I'm going with you two. I know the country east and south of these hills."

Moses shook his head, looking at me. "Ornery little woman, but hard to argue with her."

I replied, "This time she's right." I could see the carts had stopped ahead of us. "Looks like we better catch up."

CHAPTER NINETEEN

Captain Jack had finally awoken. Alexander, still mounted, was updating him on our status.

Looking to Celine as we rode up, Captain Jack announced, "Ah, there is the young lady who sewed me back together. Mrs. Munro, I give you my thanks."

He attempted to rise. "If Abigail will get me another cup of that willow bark tea, I might see myself fit to walk for a few minutes."

Celine was adamant. "Not for long though, mon capitaine! Those were very deep cuts I had to stitch. We do not want them ripping loose."

Jack turned his gaze to Moses and remarked, "Good to see you're still alive and kicking. Graham got away though?"

"For now, he did. And so did Deacon," growled Moses. "Deacon was in cahoots with him years ago when he got his hands on Hatcher's map. He hit me on the head with his rifle butt, then stole my Spencer and pistol. We will be heading out after them once we have this cart brigade out of any territory the Blackfoot claim."

I then spoke up. "Jack, the rest of the troublemakers are dead. The Gros Ventres killed them all while recovering their horses. I think we should send Milton ahead to Fort Qu'Appelle. On a good horse, he could ride hard and get there days before the carts. The Bay could send out riders to spread the word of all the shenanigans that Graham has been responsible for. It could stop, or at least slow down, the war talk. May not get everyone calmed down, but it should help avoid an all-out war."

"Yes, by all means," the captain agreed. Then, after a moment of thought, he questioned, "You don't think that traitor's going to cause more trouble?"

I replied, "No, we're pretty sure his main mission now is to get his gold back to Europe or the eastern states. He needs to get that gold to a bank. Even Canada would work if he could get east somehow. We think he's headed for the Whitemud River. He could get his hands on a canoe or a boat and go downriver to some big towns on the Missouri River. Once he deposits the gold, he can turn it into cash or a cashier's cheque. Easier to carry and hide while he travels."

Moses chimed in, "Once we get you and the brigade out of reach of the Blackfoot, we're going after Deacon. We need to be having us a discussion on the error of his ways."

The next morning, Milton left camp before sunrise, heading for Qu'Appelle. Shortly after sunup, we had the carts rolling. Moses rode out in front with Leonard while Celine and I dropped back and followed half a mile behind. It was almost like a pleasant outing for the two of us. We could just ride and enjoy each other's company.

By early afternoon, though, the weather was changing. We could see threatening clouds off in the distance behind us, getting darker and bigger the closer they came. This looked like a dangerous storm coming in, and not a little one either! The wind was picking up, and the clouds were getting blacker and starting to swirl.

Up ahead, we could see the carts turning south and heading into the hills for shelter. The cavalcade disappeared behind a hill before we caught up and followed them into a tree-lined valley. The wind was howling as the men started fighting with the oxen. We needed everything, including carts and animals, in the comparative shelter of the trees. If the stock spooked, they would be scattered for miles. All had to be hobbled or picketed with a strong rope.

Huge flashes of lightning darted across the sky, and the wind picked up even more. Soon there were branches breaking off the tops of the trees. Then the hail started falling. At least the trees offered some protection, but it was still rough on the stock as they were pelted by chunks of ice bigger than musket balls. We were shielded under the carts but were getting wet and cold.

The wind shrieked like a banshee, and the hail pounded down even harder, with the stones getting larger. I thanked our lucky stars we had made it to the coulee. I sheltered Celine with my body as best I could but felt her start to shiver.

Then, as suddenly as the storm had blown in, it abated. And all was calm again.

Crawling out from under the carts, we looked out on a desolate world. The trees were stripped of their needles and leaves, and the ground was white like it had snowed. It felt freezing cold to us, soaked as we were.

Moses yelled loud enough to get everyone's attention. "Let's get to work. We can push these carts out into the sun and get them drying while that ice melts."

We then took stock of the damage. Everything was wet. Most of the canopies on the carts had been ripped to shreds. The bags of flour, rice, and beans were soaked. All the tents were wet, but we couldn't set them up to dry on the ice. The pemmican was largely alright, as long as the rawhide bags hadn't been punctured by hailstones.

Alexander and O'Riley checked the horses. A few were bruised up some, but there seemed to be no serious injuries. The saddles had been left on the ones we had been riding, so their backs had been protected. The saddles themselves had some dents, but none were wrecked. The Sinclairs's oxen had fared the best. Being bigger than the horses and having a thicker hide had helped their cause.

As there was nowhere dry to lay him, the ladies had the captain leaning against a cart. He probably felt the cold worse than the rest of us, but never said a word. I could see why his men followed him so well.

In an hour, Leonard wanted to head out. We needed to get moving northward to find drier ground and grass for the stock. We would travel with the tents draped over the hoops of four carts so they could dry. Extra clothing and bed rolls were spread out on the hoops of the remaining carts. It was a tough pull for the oxen on the wet ground, but the carts weren't loaded heavy. By now, we'd eaten a lot of the food. With Milton riding ahead and young Paul, Jonesy Harris, and Becker Wright killed, we were four men less than when we had started out, so we left one of the tents behind. If anyone found it, they were welcome to it. We also left behind two crates of digging tools. We wouldn't be looking for dinosaurs anyway.

Fortunately, the thick-rooted sod was able to support the carts. Taking it slow and easy, we wove our way through the hills back onto the rolling prairie, angling northeast. Three hours before sunset, we reached the edge of the hail, where the grass was still standing. Soon the carts were travelling on drier ground. In another half hour, we came to a small spring. It was time to set up camp.

CHAPTER TWENTY

Between the sun and the light breeze that hung around after the storm, our tents had managed to dry. The same could not be said for the sacks of dry goods. Being packed in the carts, they were still sodden. Beans, flour, and rice were not going to dry out and be stored for future use. The only option for the flour would be to make bannock as soon as we could. The beans and rice needed to be cooked up as well. We would eat like kings until everything went mouldy or rotten.

The pemmican would last longer. It was in rawhide bags that were almost waterproof. They were hung from the carts as soon as we stopped. The exterior of the bags would soon dry off.

Once the stock had been put out to graze, Leonard and myself went on a scout. I'd make a half circle to the north, a mile out from the camp. Leonard would do the same to the south. The land was still rolling enough to hide surprises. Where we were camped, I figured the odds of someone friendly dropping by for a visit were about fifty-fifty.

I was almost at the east end of my loop when I spotted the first tracks. Dismounting, I walked across the travois and horse tracks of a large camp on the move. Looked to me they were heading south into the hills.

I was still mulling over what this could mean when Leonard rode up. He motioned towards the tracks. "You have time to figure how many Indians?"

Shaking my head, I replied, "Hard to tell because of overlap. But I'm thinkin' there are seventeen travois trails, give or take."

"That's a reasonably large camp," reflected Leonard. "I would hazard a guess there's more buffalo south. We never seen any on this side yet."

"Could even be some in the hills, making their way north," I commented. "Them buffalo would be drawing tribes from miles around."

Then something crossed my mind. "Leonard, if'n you was this renegade killer carrying some sacks of gold, would you want to meet up with any Indians? By now, he might not even find any favour from the Blackfoot. He hasn't been around them for thirty years."

Leonard nodded thoughtfully. "You have a point there. The only way he could travel and hope to avoid people would be north. A couple days' ride from the hills, and he could be at the South Saskatchewan. There's enough cottonwoods in places he could build a raft and float downriver. If he could steal a canoe somewhere along the way, it would make it quicker and easier to get to Lake Winnipeg. From the south end of the lake, he could make his way east to Canada. It would be a rough journey, but with another man to help paddle, it could be possible."

We made our way back to the carts, all the while hashing over different scenarios. If Graham threw caution to the wind and took the southern route, we were finished.

We were not going to follow him or anyone else into a buffalo hunt conducted by tribes who hated each other.

We could smell the cooking fires before we arrived back at the camp. While we were out scouting, all the able men had been gathering buffalo chips. These were year-old or older patties of buffalo manure, dry enough to burn. There had been no wood at this spring, and seeing as what little wood we carried was wet, this was the alternative.

We could see that everyone had been busy. The ladies were making all of the flour into bannock. They had even enlisted some of the soldiers as kitchen help. Every available utensil was in use. Beans were cooking in one huge pot, and rice in another. The beans and rice from the very centre of the sacks was spread out over a cloth laid out on a cart in hopes that it could be salvaged. Thankfully, the tea had been in an airtight wooden container and was still dry.

Captain Jack was starting to move around, albeit slowly. I went over to where he was leaning on a cart, talking to Moses.

"You sure you should be moving around?" I asked.

"Your wife doesn't think so. But I need to know what is going on. This seemed to be the best way. Moses tells me that you and Leonard were out scouting. Find anything of importance?"

I nodded. "We came across travois tracks, heading into the hills. Seein' as we haven't seen any buffalo, except that herd to the west, we're thinkin' the herds are making their way north, and some are coming into the hills. Could be some herds east as well. What this means to Graham is, unless he wants to take the risk of running into a lot of Indians hunting buffalo, his only option is to go north.

"I'm pretty sure them heavy sacks of gold on a horse would attract attention. By now, all the tribes know that yellow rocks are worth a lot of trade goods at any trading post. There's still a possibility we might nail your traitor yet."

Jack was quiet for a minute, then spoke. "Is there a way we could corner him? Our carts can't keep up to his horses."

"Might not have to. I doubt he had his gold yet when you had your run-in with Mr. Grizz. He will have found it by now. We have to assume it was east of where you were scratched. He was roughly a day ahead of you. We took a day to get you and Moses back to camp and a day getting to where we are now. Graham has three days on us. Two days would have gotten them into the hills, find the gold, and head south only to find it gettin' mighty crowded with Indians. If I was him, I would have turned around and headed north. A long day riding would put them somewhere east and south of us."

Moses grinned. "My Lord, Jim, I'm a'thinkin' you're on to something!"

By now, the cooking marathon was grinding to a halt. Soon, the sun would be setting. Everyone was tuckered and in need of sleep. Leonard would take first watch, I'd do middle, and Luke Sinclair would finish with the last. Crawling into our tent, I found Celine already sound asleep. She'd have tried to wait up for me, but her head wasn't fully healed yet, and today had been a trying day on us all. The pace was rough on her, Moses, and the captain, even though none of them would admit it.

After an uneventful night, the sun rose on a new day. I woke before Celine and, not wanting to disturb her, lay there quietly thinking. With Graham's men wiped out and Graham himself now on the run with his gold, we had curtailed, or hopefully even stopped, an Indian war between the tribes.

Our main concern now was tracking Graham. If he was a gambler and headed south, he was out of our hands. But if he headed north, we just might catch up to him.

And there was still the Deacon factor. He would be after that gold too. Moses was by now convinced that it was Deacon's treachery that had led to the whole episode that got Hatcher killed.

Celine opened her eyes, then smiled as she gazed up at me. "Good morning, Jim." She snuggled in closer for a minute, then sat up and declared, "When you ride out ahead today, I will be with you. You and Leonard found something last night, didn't you? I saw your face when you rode in, and I know that look."

"We did." I quickly brought her up to date about finding the travois trails as we packed our bed rolls.

Over a breakfast of bannock, fried rice, and pemmican, we discussed our options and came up with an action plan. Celine and I would ride out to the east as soon as we had finished eating. The carts would roll as soon as possible, as we still needed distance from the Blackfoot. After an hour on the trail, Moses and Leonard would start scouting out ahead of the carts. That way, if Celine and me were ahead of Graham, Moses and Leonard would come across his tracks.

We would be stopping and scanning the surrounding countryside from the hilltops whenever possible and should be able to spot either riders or tracks. I figured that if our quarry decided to head for the river, he would be trying to take the shortest route. That meant straight north from wherever they came out of the hills.

The Sinclairs would keep the carts rolling east. Even if we didn't return, they were to keep heading east to the trail up to Fort Qu'Appelle. We would eventually catch up or be on the hunt. Either way, the carts were to get well out of reach of the Blackfoot.

An hour after leaving camp, we found ourselves close to the crest of a ridge that ran north and south. Celine stayed with the horses while I crawled to a point I could scan the countryside for a few miles to the east. Nothing but dry grass.

We continued on eastward. Late afternoon, we came to a small spring-fed pond. Some Indians had stopped here a couple days ago, a small encampment with the trails of only four travois. They had watered and rested, then moved on.

Once the horses were rested, we started travelling east again. At least the weather had changed with the hail storm. It wasn't as blistering hot as it had been. But now we had some skeeters pestering us. I figured we had already covered a good thirty miles since morning. How far should we travel?

Celine had been thinking the same thing. "Jim, do you think Graham would have gone any further east before heading north?"

"I don't think so. We can make a dry camp in a buffalo waller. We'll wait to see if Moses has come across anything when he catches up to us."

Figuring the horses would give us some warning of anyone approaching, we lay down underneath the prairie stars for the night.

CHAPTER TWENTY-ONE

Two hours after sunup, Moses and Leonard rejoined us. By the looks on their faces, I didn't need to ask if they had seen any sign.

"Well," Moses grumbled, "is it worth going forward?"

"What if we go five miles farther east?" I suggested. "Then wait for a couple hours before heading back to the carts. It's possible they're travelling at night. And if that's the case, we'll come across their tracks."

The four of us headed east. At about four miles from where we spent the night, we came across a seep. We carefully checked around it to make sure it was safe, and could tell no one had stopped here in a long time. There was just enough water for us and our horses coming out of a spring at the base of a small hill. Leaving Moses and Celine with the horses, Leonard and myself climbed up the hill. Laying on the crest, we could observe the country for miles. I scanned the rolling prairie through the field glasses but saw nothing moving in any direction.

Could Graham have gambled and tried to make it to the Missouri? One new thought came to mind. If Deacon caught up with the gold, the ensuing fight should kill one of them.

I handed the glasses over to Leonard. "Take a gander. I'm not seeing anything moving out there."

Leonard peered out across the dried-out landscape for a few minutes, then whispered, "Just wait…there's something moving, Long way off though, to the east." He paused, then went on to say, "It's definitely a man on a horse. Too far away to tell who it is yet. He is travelling north, angling a little west."

Leonard returned the field glasses. Scanning to the north ahead of our rider, I could not observe any movement. "If it's Deacon, he's following tracks. I'm not seeing any activity to the north or the northwest. Let's get back to the horses."

We eased our way back down from the crest of the hill so as not to create any sudden movement. We might not be the only people with field glasses checking out the countryside.

Once we were well below the hill's crest, we scrambled back to Celine and Moses.

"Any sign of movement?" questioned Moses.

"One lone rider, heading north and angling west. Too far east to tell who it is. Or even if it's an Indian or a white man," I replied. "We'll have to get closer. I'm a thinkin' if we ride north, kind of parallel, we could maybe find another hill where we can get a better look and see if it is Deacon. Gotta be careful, though. If we can see him, there's a chance he could spot us."

"He's heading straight to the river," muttered Moses. "Almost too easy."

Leonard spoke. "He's not riding fast. We could get ahead and let him ride towards us."

"Sounds like the best way to me," I agreed.

Keeping ourselves from being silhouetted on any high ground, we made our way north. Back on the prairie, it wasn't hard to figure out why the tribes fought over the Cypress Hills. Out here on the grasslands, it was hotter, drier, and lacking shelter. Good buffalo pasture, but nowhere to overwinter. A smaller camp might be able to survive the cold in the river valleys, provided there were enough trees for firewood.

By early afternoon, we decided it was time to chance a hilltop observation. Once again, Leonard and myself crawled to the crest. We could see for miles across the prairie. At least the higher spots. Even to the east, where it looked flatter, it wasn't. I've heard that farther east and south, there is a big plain that is flat for miles. That's definitely not the way it is this far north. If our rider wasn't wanting to be noticed, he could weave his way north as we had. Only if it was Deacon, he would be tracking someone. And that someone was making a beeline to the South Saskatchewan River within a day's ride either side of the Forks.

Looking southeast through the field glasses, I started scanning the horizon. This wasn't as easy as it sounds. The heat was causing a shimmering effect. Off in the distance, nothing was very clear. Watching to the southeast for a few minutes, I could see nothing. Then, there was something in the haze. Handing the glasses to Leonard, I pointed to where I thought I'd seen movement. "Can you make anything out?"

Leonard was silent for a good two minutes. Then he slowly spoke. "Rider just came into view again from behind a hill. He's about a mile east and a mile south of us."

Turning around and scanning the terrain to the north and east, Leonard nodded. "It wouldn't be hard to get in front of him. We could follow the lay of the land north on our side of this hill. We stay to the low ground, then cut east on the north side of that rolling ridge."

"Sounds good. We better get going." We started back down the hill to where Celine and Moses were waiting.

"We've gotta get riding now! I'll explain on our way," I said in a low voice as I swung up on my horse.

Following the contour of the land, we were able to stay out of sight while stalking who we hoped was Deacon. Travelling as fast as we dared, for fear of making dust, we were soon where we needed to turn to cut off the rider.

There was a light breeze at our backs as we rode east in silence. That worked in our favour. If it was from the north, the rider's horse would smell us and give us away. As it was, our horses wouldn't smell his either.

I glanced at Celine. She met my gaze with a hurried smile that did nothing to hide the stress she was feeling.

Moses had a look of determination on his face, but I could see more in his eyes. Half a lifetime of hunting to avenge his friend was starting to come to a head. Deacon could well have been the catalyst leading to Hatcher's death. We get Deacon, then we get after this Graham. The gold would be a bonus.

Leonard raised his arm, signalling us to halt. Looking behind us, I could see we had almost covered a mile since our turn eastward.

Silently, we all dismounted and landed our horses to Celine. This time, she didn't argue.

Leonard was carrying his Reb sniper rifle, I had my Spencer, while Moses had his old Nazareth. If it was

Deacon, hopefully we could take him without a shot. We needed him alive to answer some questions.

After giving Celine a wink and a smile, I followed the other two. Dropping to the ground before we crested the hill, I pointed to Leonard and nodded. He crawled until he could peek over the crest of the hill. A quick look, and he immediately came back to us.

Whispering, he declared, "It's Deacon. And he's coming towards us. Should top the hill a few yards left of us."

"Good." A low growl came from Moses. "I'll move up the hill, staying just below the crest. Leonard, move around behind me to the left about ten yards. Be ready to drop him if he bolts east, south, or west. Drop the horse if you have to. Jim, stay about ten yards downhill from me. If he bolts north, you take him."

We took up our positions. There were always so many things that could go wrong. What if he angled off and didn't come over the rise anywhere near us? The waiting was always the worst.

We were all ready to spring when the horse walked over the crest. With no rider!

I rolled and was immediately on my feet as a gun fired and a bullet whined over my head. Running downhill, I could hear a loud blast from Moses's old mountain rifle.

By the time I was at the base of the ridge, Deacon was pointing Moses's stolen Spencer at my wife. I could see the fire in her eyes. If looks could kill, he'd already be dead.

He walked towards her, hollering, "I'm gonna take this little lady with me as insurance. And your horses. Put your guns down, or I'll take my chances and shoot her now."

"Okay, we'll do it," I yelled at him. "But if you hurt her, you'll die slow." I knelt down to set my carbine on the ground and saw Celine nod ever so slightly. Behind me, I heard Moses and Leonard lay their guns down. Once the guns were on the ground, I could sense Deacon relax a little. Celine noticed as well, and she winked at me. I was in the process of rising when she dropped and rolled. Deacon fired a shot that went into a horse's chest as my first pistol ball drilled into his belly, followed by two more.

The carbine fell from his hand on the second one, but I'd committed to three shots in my mind.

I ran over to Celine and threw my arms around her. "My Lord, woman, that was close."

She was still shaking. "I knew he'd kill me if he took me with him. He is truly evil." Then, looking at me, she continued, "I figured he had never seen anyone as fast with a pistol as you. I knew you wouldn't let him take me."

By now, Moses was standing over Deacon. "Looks to me like your horse thievin' days are over. You're gut shot. I bet you never seen a man before who could draw and shoot a pistol like my grandson."

Then his voice darkened. "It was you who told that Hudson Bay renegade about Hatcher's map and the gold, wasn't it? I remember catchin' you diggin' through Hatcher's pack. But I caught you before you could steal it.

"I'm thinkin' you met up with that black-hearted bastard at rendezvous. You told him about the gold and the map that Hatcher would have on him. You let Graham know where we would winter. And where, in all likelihood, we would do our spring trapping.

"Do you know how Smiley and Hatcher died? Was that part of your plan too? Graham tortured them to make them reveal where the valley with the gold was. They didn't even know which mountain valley or stream it was in." He paused, then spat out in disgust, "And Hatcher was your kin, too."

"Oh God, I hurt," moaned Deacon.

"Graham was just supposed to steal the map. I didn't know he would torture them. He betrayed me too. I caught up with him later in the summer, like we planned. It took us two years to find that gold." His voice was getting weaker, as was his breath. "When we finally found it, he shot me. I barely got away. He double-crossed me, then got himself another partner and disappeared with the gold!"

Struggling to breathe, Deacon whined, "I just wanted to get my share of the gold. Hatcher and Smiley been dead for over thirty-five years. It don't matter now." Then his head slumped sideways, and his eyes quit blinking.

With tears in his eyes, Moses looked down at the dead man and declared, "Smiley and Hatcher mattered to *me*, you evil, treacherous bastard. Here's hoping the devil has a busy night planned for you."

"And I'll be taking my carbine and pistol back too," Moses snarled.

Moses slowly walked a short distance from us to be alone. Leaving Celine to keep an eye on him, Leonard and myself set about catching our horses. Celine had to let go of them when she dropped and rolled away from Deacon. Fortunately, we were able to catch all three of ours, as well as Deacon's. Leonard would be acquiring Deacon's horse, as his had been the one shot.

I approached Moses, who was still standing off to himself. "We're ready to ride. Leonard found tracks of three horses only twenty yards east of us. They look to be a day old or less. It's got to be Graham."

The old man nodded. "I should never have let Smiley go off with Hatcher. We should've just made Smiley and Dexter settle their differences over that woman. If I'd a been with Hatch, I might've noticed them Blackfeet coming at us. Smiley was a good man and hell on wheels in a close-up fight. But he was bordering on near-sighted. He couldn't make out a man on a horse a mile away."

He finally looked up at me. "Jim, I blame myself for almost getting Celine killed. I should've known that Deacon would be on to us. Lord knows he was a treacherous bastard, but he was one hell of a mountain man and horse thief. No one had ever got the jump on him."

Then, straightening, he turned towards the horses. "Let's finish this. We're still lawmen. That murdering renegade won't get away from me a second time."

As we mounted, I shuddered to think how close I had come to losing Celine. I resolved that, until this was over, one of the three of us would be with her at all times. We had a lot of living to do yet.

CHAPTER TWENTY-TWO

Picking up the trail was easy, as Graham was making no effort to hide his tracks. He was heading north and slightly west. Earlier, we had all figured he would head for the Forks or even east to get to the river. This trail was going to bring him up to the South Saskatchewan, well west of the Forks.

It was Leonard who realized where our quarry was going. Looking ahead in the direction the tracks were heading, he commented, "He's heading to a ford on the South Saskatchewan. I remember my cousin telling me there was a crossing west of the Forks. It was where the river starts to gradually curve more southerly. He said it wasn't a full day's ride from where they camped. Be less than two days from the Forks."

"What in tarnation is he up to?" questioned Moses.

"Trees," answered Leonard. "He needs trees to build a raft and there are some close to the crossing. This is a less travelled route and not on any cart trail. Less chance of anyone coming along, except Blackfoot. When Palliser went through in '59, there were two Blood camps just west a day or so from the crossing. They won't likely be around unless some buffalo moved into the area while we were in the hills. We've been lucky so far, but if we keep after this Graham, we gotta keep our eyes peeled in all four directions."

"I'm going after that torturing bastard," growled Moses. "You young folks better get back to the carts. There's no need for you to have a run-in with the Blackfeet."

"I'm not leaving you to go it alone. I'm with you," I declared.

"And where Jim goes, I go!" insisted Celine.

Leonard laughed. "For a bunch of farmers, you Munros sure don't go out of your way to avoid trouble. Reckon I better stick with you. You might be needin' a hand to finish this."

We were riding our horses hard and couldn't keep up this pace much longer. Not having remounts, our horses were going to need time to rest and graze. At a small seep, we took a break to water the horses and let them grab a few mouthfuls of the dried-out grass.

While chewing on some pemmican, I voiced my opinion. "We have one chance to catch up. Our horses could be pushed for part of the night. That might just get us close enough to get a shot at him. If we don't catch him tonight, our horses are done for. Then we'll have to rest them for a day or more. But we can figure his horses are tiring as well. If he stops for the night, we could just catch up and take him. If'n he gets to the river, it won't take long to throw a raft together. Then he's gone. We could try to catch him, but the odds ain't that good."

Moses nodded. "It could work. Worth a try. If it doesn't work, we could head east once the horses have a rest." Then, looking at Leonard, he said, "How would he get to civilization goin' east on rivers? Someone at a Hudson Bay port might recognize him. And how often do ships even arrive?"

"I think his best bet would be to use the old canoe routes to Montreal, the way the old Nor'Westers came west to trade. Iffy, but doable. Need two men and a light canoe. The portages are the worst part. I'm thinkin' he's doing his plannin' on the fly. Them buffalo and Indians south of the hills kinda wrecked his getaway on the southern rivers."

"So we need to catch him before he gets on the water. Or he'll get away from us." I looked at my tired partners. "Are you up for pushing on?"

"There will be some moonlight tonight," commented Leonard. "That'll help."

Celine suggested, "We could walk for a few minutes of every hour. It would help the horses, and we would still gain."

Moses nodded in approval. "Good idea."

Although Moses and Celine were both determined to see this through, I had my reservations. Neither one was fully recovered yet, and they would need to be resting. Even more so than the horses.

We rode and walked until the sun was setting. We stopped in a low depression that had some green grass, then unsaddled and picketed the horses for an hour. Moses and Celine grabbed some sleep. Not enough, but it might help them get through the coming night.

When the hour was up, we hit the trail again. Fortunately, we were heading into a slight breeze as we set out. This was a stroke of good luck on our part. This was hilly country we were travelling in. Our horses would let us know if we got close to Graham and company.

Following the tracks of three horses by moonlight wasn't hard in the light, dry soil. After our second rest stop, the ground started to slope to the northeast.

"We are approaching the river," whispered Leonard. "There are long ravines that come out at the water. We need to watch for rattlesnakes. My cousin said this place was crawling with them. Being this hot, they will be hunting at night."

As Leonard had warned us, the landscape suddenly changed. Arroyos branched into the deep coulee from the prairie. Carefully, we followed the tracks down into the long ravine with barren sides. From the top, it looked like we were at least half a mile from the river. Fighting down the urge to move a little faster, we slowly picked our way in the moonlight, each step getting us closer to our quarry.

Then the rattling started! The horse I was on was a prairie born and bred mustang. He stopped in his tracks. Easing back on the lines, I whispered soothingly, "Back, back, back up," which happened to be just what that horse instinctively wanted to do. Once we backed away a few steps, the rattling stopped.

Making a slight course change, I continued to lead us towards the river. A half hour later, we were watching the South Saskatchewan flow by on its way to Lake Winnipeg.

Celine had cupped her hands to her ears. "I can faintly hear somebody cutting on trees with an axe or, more likely, a tomahawk," she said in a low voice.

"Let's get across this river then. Hopefully, they're so busy they don't notice us," murmured Moses.

It wasn't the worst river crossing we had ever conducted. At least the water was shallow enough that our guns didn't get wet.

Once across, we made our way downstream towards the trees. I held up my arm. Once everyone was beside me, I pointed to the river bank a hundred yards ahead of us. By the light of the moon, we could make out the shapes of fresh-cut logs that had been dragged to the edge. It wouldn't take very many more and some rope to fashion a raft. Crude, but it would serve the purpose until they could steal a canoe.

I spoke quietly. "Let's just wait here. When they bring more logs, we'll take 'em out." I strained to see in the darkness. "No sign of the gold. It must be back with them where they're cutting."

We led our horses back a ways, finding a place to tie them where they would be out of sight and far enough away they wouldn't be heard.

A few minutes later, a man appeared, dragging a log. He set it alongside the others, then turned and disappeared back into the brush.

"I'll take him when he brings the next log," Moses hissed and silently began moving towards where the man had vanished. The three of us stayed in place. Moses would need no help taking out one man.

Roughly fifteen minutes later, we heard a small scuffle, and then all was quiet. We heard a soft rustling, and then Moses came into sight, dragging a man by his feet. Leonard and I met him and took over. Once we had the jasper's dead body hidden out of sight, we set out to get Graham.

Celine and Leonard were left behind to watch the river shoreline in case Graham showed up. There was always a slight chance there was another trail he could take to the river. Moses and myself slipped into the brush and followed the path the logs had been hauled on. Moving silently, we closed in on where the trees were being cut. Soon, a man was faintly visible in a small clearing.

Suddenly, he spun around, hurling the hatchet at us! What warned him, I have no idea. We both instinctively dropped, me to the left and Moses to the right. A loud roar and a sheet of flame shot out towards us. I felt the sting of a rifle ball high on my left arm.

Off to my right, I heard Moses fire his Spencer. A shot came from the trees ahead of us, and I opened up with my carbine towards the flame, firing four shots. I quickly rolled just as a hail of pistol balls covered the area around me. That bloody renegade was good! But there were two of us. While he was firing at me, Moses emptied his pistol towards the muzzle blasts. There was a thump of a bullet hitting flesh. And then the sound of someone trying to run through the trees.

We waited. "You alright?" I called to Moses in a hushed voice.

"Yeah, just a little nick on a leg. I'll wrap it quick. Pretty sure I hit him, too, by the sound of it.

"The sun is starting to show some light. It'll be peeking above the horizon in a few minutes. Then we can follow him."

While he was speaking, I had already started reloading my Leech and Rigdon. After Moses had wrapped his handkerchief around his wound, I heard him loading as well. By the time our pistols and carbines were ready, there was a little more light coming from the east. We cautiously made our way to the spot where our enemy had been shooting from.

Beside a splotch of blood lay a mountain rifle. It was similar to Moses's old Nazareth, but the furniture was brass, and it was still a flintlock. This was a nice rifle. Moses was eyeing it when he suddenly pushed me to the ground just before a pistol ball passed over us.

I rolled left again and Moses stayed where we landed.

"I never gave up hope I'd get the pleasure of killin' you!" snarled Moses.

"I should have let them Blackfoot go after you and get your scalp, you white-haired bastard. When my shot-up war party returned to camp last week, saying they had a run-in with an old man with long white hair, I knew it was you, 'Ree Killer. But this time, I'll put you under. And that gold will be all mine!" shrieked Graham.

"You ain't leavin' here. Gold or no gold. This ends here, today. The devil's been waiting a long time, and he'll be stokin' up the fires right now, gittin' Hell all nice and toasty for ya," taunted Moses.

Graham cackled. "It'll be you makin' his acquaintance today, 'Ree Killer!"

My mind was racing. Keep him talking a little more, Moses. I'm getting closer to him.

At that minute, the light breeze picked up for a few seconds, and an eerie whistling passed through the trees.

"You hear that?" bellowed Moses. "Ol' Lucifer is a callin' for ya!"

All this time, I had been crawling through the trees, making my way around behind the killer. Just keep him talking, Moses, I said to myself. By now, I could see where

Graham was hiding in the shadows on the edge of the trees, just thirty feet from me! A few more seconds was all I needed.

A loud sharp crack of a pistol and a ball thudded into a tree beside my head. I blinked my eyes, then saw a pistol barrel pointing at me! By reflex, I instantly rolled right. Firing my pistol as I quit moving, I emptied it towards him. I hit him. But this man could absorb lead!

I rolled back for my carbine. I spun around, looking for Graham. His pistol was in his belt, and he was dragging two heavy sacks, one in each hand, towards a ravine. His horses must be grazing there. He wasn't gonna give up easy!

Looking right, I could see Moses coming out of the trees. He followed Graham while I scrambled up the side of the ravine to get ahead. In a few minutes, I was with his horses, waiting.

I could see the crazed look in his eyes as he staggered towards me, dragging his gold. He stopped for a minute, fighting to get his breath. I trained my carbine on him.

Moses was walking up behind him. "I've waited a long time for this," growled Moses as he approached his nemesis.

At that moment, I noticed a small hole in the ground just in front of Graham. There was a small snake disappearing into it.

The old gold-obsessed killer turned around at the sound of Moses's voice and stepped back. He dropped one of the sacks and clawed for his pistol. Suddenly, with no warning, the ground gave way. Graham and the gold dropped out of sight into a snake pit. Then, the ominous rattling of rattlesnakes—lots of them—and screams of agony echoed from deep within the ground.

Soon, it was quiet, save for the occasional rattle.

Staying well back from the gaping hole, Moses drily commented, "Guess the devil got tired of waitin' for me to kill him."

I followed his gaze and couldn't help but mention, "Reckon the Devil has the gold too."

"He's welcome to it," Moses declared. "It was cursed from the get-go. That old Blackfoot medicine man all them years ago understood that. It's why he put it back in the ground. Everyone who ever chased after it or held it is dead. Let the devil keep it. It's his gold anyway."

We led Graham's horses back through the trees, stopping to pick up the old mountain rifle that he had left on the ground to bait us into his ambush. We met Celine and Leonard coming towards us. I drew Celine into a deep hug and held her close. "Girl, we gotta find us a safer line of work."

Our hunt was over.

CHAPTER TWENTY-THREE

The four of us mounted up and headed back across the river. We rode until we came to a secluded grassy place by the river. With a couple of days rest for ourselves, and for the seven horses, we could then head east and catch up to the carts. In a few weeks, we could be in Fort Garry, back with the rest of our family.

Once the horses were picketed, Moses stood off by himself with the brass-furnished rifle, holding it and staring off into the past. Then, with a sigh, he turned and carried the rifle over to me and Celine.

He started speaking. "Hatcher weren't like a lot of us in the mountains. I went west to make money, for sure. But it was mostly for the adventure. Finding out what was on the other side of the mountain. Livin' free to do as I pleased. Seein' as much country as possible. Hell, I even joined my Shoshone friends one time on a horse stealin' raid from the Lakota! I was out there to live.

"Hatch was out there to earn enough money to set himself up in a gun shop of his own. There was two older brothers who took over his dad's shop. Not enough business to feed all three families.

"Hatch had a wife and a son staying in Saint Louis while he was trapping. He had asked me, if anything ever happened to him, to sell what furs he had and then take the money to them. After Hatch was murdered and the spring trappin' season was over, I set out down the Missouri on a bull boat with mine and Hatcher's furs. Had quite a time gettin' down the river and keepin' my hair. Got a good price for them furs in Saint Louis, though. I threw in half of my money to make sure the widow and boy could get by."

He handed me the old rifle. "It's still a beautiful rifle. It's a flint gun, never converted to cap, but it always fired. And I never knew it to ever have a pan flash. I'm pretty sure Hatch would want you to have it."

"Why me?" I asked.

"Because he built this gun himself." The old man paused as tears formed in his eyes, and he solemnly continued, "And he was your blood grandfather."

I stared at Moses incredulously. "You mean Hatch was Pa's father?!"

Moses nodded. "And your grandma was his wife.

"Hatch was the best friend I ever had. I still have nightmares about that terrible day he died. I figgered the least I could do was look out for his wife and his son.

"I sure never planned on marryin' his widow. But sometimes, good things do come from bad. Marryin' your grandma was the best thing ever happened to me. It gave me a purpose. And a family."

Celine and I each put an arm around Moses. "You will always be our grandfather!"

Moses smiled. "I know that. But it'd be alright to remember Hatcher, too. Now let's go get some rest."

Leonard and I took turns on watch while Moses, Celine, and the horses rested up. Our good luck held as we were left undisturbed. With the buffalo being west and south of the hills, we never seen any Blackfoot. We even had the luxury of cleaning up in the cool, refreshing river.

It was while we were packing up such as we had that Leonard walked back to us. He had the morning watch and had been wandering around some fifty yards from camp.

"Moses," he called out. "Did your friend who guided Hayden ever tell you what them dinosaurs look like?"

Moses replied, "Said they kind of look like skeleton bones, but they're rock. Why you askin'?"

"Come with me. I'll show you."

We all followed Leonard around a little bend and climbed a few feet up the barren slope. There it was! Just barely visible was the side of a head, bigger than a buffalo, with long, jagged teeth. To the right a few feet were what looked to be some pretty big rib bones.

Moses started to chuckle. One by one, we joined in until we were all laughing so hard our sides ached. After all we had been through, there actually was a dinosaur out here!

Still chortling, Moses remarked, "Just wait until we tell Professor Sir John Jacob Augustus Martindale the Third about this!"

Epilogue — Somewhere On The South Saskatchewan River East Of The Forks — 1882

An old man with long white hair sat on a rocking chair on the veranda. He'd helped build this ranch house from logs that had floated down the river. Turning his gaze to the horse corrals, he smiled. My Lord, they did it. His three great-grandsons had caught a yearling for each of them.

He'd told them if they could catch a horse, they could keep it. They hadn't done too bad either. Picked the best three in the pen. The twins, William and Moses, all of fourteen this year, were shaping up to be pretty good hands. Their shadow, young Hatcher, age twelve, was a natural-born rider.

Looking around the ranch yard, he could see his son, William Sr., and his grandson, Jim, had just arrived home and were putting their saddle horses away in the barn. They'd just returned from selling some horses to the Mounted Police at Fort Walsh.

He sure missed seein' Judith and Ollie and their young'uns. Maybe when that new railroad they was a buildin' reached the Cypress Hills, he could take Grandma back east to Winnipeg for a visit.

By the mouthwatering smells drifting through the air from the kitchen, he judged Celine and Grandma would be havin' supper ready soon.

Standing up to go into the house, he turned and paused. Looking out to the southwest, he thought to himself Hatch would be mighty pleased with how his family had turned out. It was quite a legacy.

THE END